THE REAPER

Published by Boson Books

An imprint of Bitingduck Press

Formerly an imprint of C&M Online Media, Inc.

ISBN 978-1-932482-56-0

eISBN 978-1-932482-57-7

For information contact

Bitingduck Press, LLC

Altadena, CA

notifications@bitingduckpress.com

http://www.bitingduckpress.com

Author's note

This book is a work of fiction with a historical backdrop. I have taken liberties with historical figures, ships, and time frames to blend in with my story. Therefore, this book is not a reflection of actual historical events.

THE REAPER

THE FIGHTING ANTHONYS
BOOK ONE

MICHAEL AYE

REVISED 2017

Books by Michael Aye

Fiction

War of 1812 Trilogy

War of 1812: Remember the Raisin, Book 1

Battle at Horseshoe Bend, Book 2

The Fighting Anthonys
The Reaper, Book One
HMS SeaWolf, Book Two
Barracuda, Book Three
SeaHorse, Book Four
Peregrine, Book Five
Trident, Book Six
Leopard, Book Seven

The Pyrate Trilogy
Pyrate, The Rise of Cooper Cain, Book One

I must go down to the sea
To the lonely sea and the sky
And all I ask is a tall ship
And a star to steer her by
... John Masefield

Prologue

"Fire! Fire as you bear."

"Damme Sir, but this is hot work!"

"Not too hot for your taste is it, Mr. Buck?"

The first lieutenant turned to his captain, "Nay Captain, but it's close."

A huge splinter cut through the air, making a whooshing sound as it barely missed Buck's head. Involuntarily he ducked. "Aye, Captain, it's close!"

"Mr. Trent's respects, sir!"

"Yes, Mr. Dean!"

"There's two pirates approaching aft, sir, as if they intend to grapple and board."

"Two pirates, Mr. Dean?"

"Ere, two galleys o' pirates, sir."

"Very well!" Captain Gilbert Anthony answered. "Mr. Buck, reinforce aft if you please!"

"Aye, Captain, we'll attend the whoresons. Come along now, Mr. Dean, and do be careful. Your father would never forgive me if I was to send you home in halves."

"Yes, sir," the midshipman answered with the hint of a smile on his face.

Chapter One

THE CARRIAGE LURCHED AND seemed to twist as it hit yet another pothole. The sudden jolt broke Anthony's train of thought and felt like it damned near broke some of his aching bones. Was it only four, no six, weeks ago that he had brought *HMS Recourse*, a thirty-two gun frigate, limping into Portsmouth Harbour? They had repaired as much damage as possible, but the scars of battle were still obvious to all. "*Damme, what a fight that had been,*" Anthony thought.

Recourse had been headed home to England when Peckham, the keen old master, commented to those officers around him on the quarterdeck, "I hear cannon fire."

No sooner were the words out of Peckham's mouth than the lookout called down, "Deck thar! Looks like several galleys attacking a convoy, sir!"

Once *Recourse* waded in, the Honourable East India Company's fat merchant ships took advantage of their luck and showed their heels as they sailed for safer waters. *Recourse's* entry surprised the pirates as well. They thought they only had to deal with a lone escort, making the convoy easy pickings. The escort was a ten gun sloop of war.

She had bared her fangs like a feisty dog, but was doomed until *Recourse* showed up with her guns blazing.

Little did Anthony know that one action could set into motion a course of events that would change his life forever. Looking back, several things had happened so fast that it seemed a blur...a dream, from which he was just awakening.

As he gazed out the carriage window at the dreary countryside, he wondered where the wind and tides would take him. An Admiralty messenger had come aboard as soon as *Recourse* had moored in Portsmouth Harbour. Anthony was swiftly escorted to the Admiralty for a quick interview with Lord Sandwich, the First Lord. Lord Sandwich then took the new hero in tow as they rushed off to a celebration given by the Honourable East India Company in recognition of Anthony's daring action. One of the directors got up and read the article that had been sent to *The Gazette*. The article was overly lavish in the telling of the bravery and honor demonstrated by *Recourse's* captain and crew. Much was made of Captain Anthony being the son of Fighting James Anthony, Vice Admiral of the Red. The speaker ended, declaring, "It appears we have another Fighting Anthony."

After the speech, the speaker then turned the presentation over to Hugh English, Anthony's brother-in-law.

"Captain Anthony—Gil, as a small token of our esteemed gratitude I would like to offer you a small reward." He then handed a purse full of gold coins to Anthony. As soon as Anthony accepted the coins, Hugh continued, "I would also like to present you with this ceremonial sword from Wilkinson's."

As Anthony set down the bag of coins to accept the sword, he couldn't help but ponder the remark about a small token of their appreciation. The sword was worth at least a hundred guineas and the reward was certainly nice. There had been no thought of a reward when Anthony put *Recourse* into the midst of the fight. However, he couldn't help but think that their rewards were indeed just a token. One only had to look at what it would cost to replace a ship, not to mention the added cost of the cargo, had the pirates had their way. A small token indeed.

Anthony was also sure Hugh had something to do with the celebration and reward. Hugh's father had been a merchant captain for the Honest John's, as the Honourable East India Company was commonly called. Hugh was now one of the company's directors, a Member of Parliament, as well as a close friend to the Prince Regent.

Anthony was certain his sudden bestowal of knighthood was stimulated by Hugh's relationship with the Prince. The ceremony happened quickly, with the First Lord escorting Anthony to his Majesty King George's chamber. Along the way, he had whispered hurried instructions to Gil so that he would not embarrass the family name or the Navy. The episode was such a blur that Anthony could barely recall the events. He remembered kneeling before the King, who said a handful of words that Anthony couldn't remember, and then he was dubbed "Sir Gilbert, Knight of the Bath." As soon as he had been dubbed and congratulated, he was quickly whisked away, as more important affairs were in need of his Majesty's attention.

***

PLEADING ILLNESS, ANTHONY'S FATHER had not been present for either the Honest John's celebration or the knighting, but he sent his love.

Then came the summons. A messenger had brought word that Gil's father was in critical health; this was the reason for Anthony's hurried journey home. The driver cracked his whip as the horses labored to keep up a quickened pace as they fought the howling wind and snow.

Gil's father, Lord James Anthony, Earl of Deerfield, had been a Vice Admiral of some standing, making a name for himself equal to Anson and Hawke. He had distinguished himself at Cape Finisterre and Quiberon Bay, earning himself the nickname Fighting James Anthony. However, an ailing marriage and politics had caused Lord Anthony to haul down his flag prematurely.

Gil's mother lived in Kent on the family estate with her cats and "medicinal" brandy. Becky, his sister, with the help of a good overseer, took care of their mother and Deerfield.

Admiral Lord Anthony had turned his back on it all, saying, "a man should not tarry in a place where never blows a fair wind." He had kept in touch with his children, and they had visited with their father in secret. They had once told their mother of these visits, and it was then that Gil found the true meaning of "a foul wind."

Gil had once questioned his father as to the reason for the separation from his mother. Lord Anthony's only remark was that some things were better left alone. The matter was never mentioned again. Lord Anthony had moved to Portsmouth and bought a townhouse where he could peer out the second floor windows, or sit on a balcony and see the ships and the harbour. He also acquired a mistress named Maria, a gypsy woman, with eyes and hair as black as the darkest night. She was twenty years younger than Lord Anthony, but their life had been happy regardless of their age difference. Maria was seductive without trying. She was elegant and possessed a quiet humor that made liking her easy. Not wanting to be disloyal to his mother, Gil still had to admit his father had been a lucky man to have shared his life with Maria. It was very obvious she was totally devoted to Lord Anthony.

***

FATHER HAD NEVER BEEN sick to Gil's recollection, however, he was now seventy-eight years old. He had looked so robust just a year ago, but this was not the case any longer.

Upon entering his father's home, Gil was shocked at the appearance of the man before him. His decline in health was appalling. Nothing was familiar except the hand- carved meerschaum pipe his father had clenched between his teeth. Through calm seas and cannon balls, that pipe had always been there. Now the shell that had once been a robust man held it tightly.

Upon entering his father's room, Gil could see his father's eyes light up. The fire was dimmed but not out. His father's rough Scottish accent was still plain as he spoke, the voice still commanding, though not as strong as it once was.

"I'm glad ye made it. I was about to have this lawyer set things down on paper the way I want them to be. I still will, so that there'll be a record, jus' in case something should happen to me sudden like. I pray not, but it could."

Gil nodded his greeting to the barrister. Lord Anthony paused to catch his breath, and then started speaking again. "Now I can see ye be ripe and bursting with questions, son. However, I ask ye to hold 'em for now, cause my breath is short. There are things that have to be said and agreed upon. You can ask questions later if I'm still with the living."

Gil nodded his willingness to do as his father requested, thinking all the time that he was still acting like an admiral, in command right up to the end. Lord Anthony called Maria into the room. She came in and sat on the arm of the chair next to him. His father resumed his conversation once Maria was settled.

"You know Maria has been my life for twenty years. I would have married her had there been a way. But it was not to be. Your mother's family had more influence with the church than I did, so my petition for a divorce was never granted. When I'm gone, this house is to be hers along with a trust I've set aside. You probably guessed all this, but what you don't know, Gil, is that you have a brother."

The barrister suddenly found an extra burst of energy; his quill flew over the paper as he wrote down this new information.

"Our son has been named after his grandfathers. He's been entered in my Bible as Gabriel Marcus Anthony. Poor as some may think it, I do want him to share in what little status the name may make in regards to his birthright. I want you, as my eldest son, the son who'll inherit my title and all of Deerfield, to give me your word that my wishes will be carried out – that Gabe will be accepted as an Anthony. Do I have your word on this, my son?" Lord James Anthony could barely hold back the tears as he asked for his son's promise.

"Aye, Father, you have my vow," Gil answered with a quaver in his voice and a renewed sense of compassion and love for the man who sat before him. A deep sigh of relief escaped the old man.

Pausing long enough to catch his breath again, Lord Anthony continued, but his voice was weaker, and Gil grew concerned, though still refusing to interrupt his father. "Your brother is a midshipman. He's spent four years with Captain Suckling on *Raisonnable*, and the last two years, he's been on a revenue cutter. His papers are all in order. I've taught him navigation and seamanship. All he needs is another year or so with a good captain...someone to teach him what it really means to command. I taught ye well enough, I'd like to think. Now I want you to teach him. In a year he'll be ready to sit for the lieutenant's exam." The last was said with a strain as his breath grew weaker.

***

VICE ADMIRAL LORD JAMES Anthony died two days later. Gil was overwhelmed with emotion as his father's friends and shipmates turned out for the funeral. Despite the icy rain mixed with snow, people braved the cold to pay their last respects. When the chapel had filled, people stood in the freezing slush till the service had ended. Even Lord Sandwich, the First Lord of the Admiralty, attended.

Gil's sister, Becky, and her husband Hugh were there with their little girl, Gretchen. Gil thought her the most spoiled little nit he'd ever seen. Maria was there with Gabe. It was the first time Gil had a chance to meet his brother. Looking at Maria during the eulogy, Gil could see the toll his father's illness and death had taken on her, and he couldn't help but feel kindly toward her. She had given herself totally to his father, but to some she would always be just Lord Anthony's mistress. Gil would never forget the look of relief in her eyes when he embraced her at the gravesite and kissed her hand. He wanted her to know she would always be special to him. The First Lord had given him a flag on behalf of the nation in honour of his father. Gil in turn gave it to Maria. She deserved it much more than he did.

After the funeral, Gil approached Becky and Hugh. "I see mother didn't attend."

"Did you expect her to?" Becky replied.

"No, but I wasn't sure."

"Well, it was probably better for all present that she didn't," Hugh added as he gazed over at Maria and Gabe.

Chapter Two

THE DAMPNESS SEEMED TO fill the coach. Gil Anthony pulled his boat cloak more tightly about him, yet he was unable to prevent a shudder as a gust of wind penetrated the confines of the coach, sending a chill right through him. The sun had all but set, and with its setting, the air would grow much colder. Anthony knew they still had a long journey before they reached London and it was going to be most uncomfortable. Gabe sat across from him. Slumped in his seat, Gabe appeared to be dozing. The two had talked little since the funeral. Gil detected an air of anger about the boy and was not sure of its origin. Was it due to the fact that his birth had not benefited from a proper wedding? He had his mother's good looks, her darkness and her eyes, but everything else was his father's. His laughs were quick, but Gil was betting his temper would be quicker. He was quiet, but seemed to have wit. He also seemed very suspicious, yet under the circumstances, who wouldn't be? How many times had he been called the Admiral's bastard behind his back? How many times had he heard? Could this be why he seemed so guarded and quick to anger?

Anthony had given his word to his dying father to take Gabe under his wing and make him a sea officer. This was a promise he didn't take lightly. However, he wondered how the relationship would play out. *Will I be able to accept Gabe, not only as a midshipman but also as a brother? Will Gabe accept me?*

Anthony hoped the summons from the Admiralty would be to receive orders, hopefully command of another ship, something to get him away. He needed the sea. While some men detested life aboard ship, he found comfort in its confines. Lord Anthony, Gil's father, had discussed this love for the sea with him many times.

"Gil, ye were born with salt water in ye veins," Father had joked. Thinking of his father made Gil think of the messenger who had carried the urgent news of Lord Anthony's ill health.

The messenger, Dagan, was a mystery. He was Maria's younger brother and Gabe's uncle. Anthony had guessed him to be in his mid to late twenties, but he seemed much older for some reason. At Lord Anthony's funeral, Dagan was always close to Gabe, like a protective angel or bodyguard. Yet he was at Maria's hand whenever she needed him. The girl servants all seemed moonstruck when he was around. A few even looked upon him in a mischievous, tempting manner.

"He puts a spell on 'em he does," their father, Lord Anthony, had said half jokingly before his death.

The male servants were all polite but distant, seeming overly cautious when Dagan was about. In a hurried whisper, one of Lord Anthony's long time personal servants, a seaman who'd sailed with the old admiral, had warned Anthony, "Be careful like, zur, 'e sees the future, 'e does. 'E talks to the ravens, aye zur. Seen 'im at it, I have." Fearing he'd be overheard, the old servant was so close Anthony could feel the man's hot breath on his ear as he whispered in a barely audible voice. "E's a soothsayer, zur, maybe 'e's even a sorcerer."

"Huh," snorted Anthony. His father had proclaimed Dagan a "damn'd fine seaman."

"We'll have to see about him being a sorcerer."

Anthony had also been told of "The Vow." Maria's father would normally have been Gabe's protector and confidant, according to gypsy custom.

However, since the death of Maria and Dagan's father, Dagan had taken his place by completing some ritual, and he was now Gabe's protector. Therefore, wherever goeth Gabe, goeth Dagan, as long as he lived. Anthony had no doubt that Dagan would fulfill his vow of protection.

Anthony was sure this vow was behind their father's desire for Gabe to be under his command.

"You're getting a bargain," Lord James Anthony had said just before he died. "Besides being a fine topman, Dagan's got the best peepers I've ever seen."

***

THE COACH RATTLED ALONG toward Whitehall. Even at such an early hour the street was no longer deserted and appeared to be coming alive before Anthony and Gabe's eyes. The coach's driver let loose a stream of curses aimed at a pie-man who hadn't moved his cart out of the coach's way quick enough to suit the driver.

"Too fat and slow 'e is, like as not 'e's been eating 'is own wares I'd say, damn 'im."

A mob of ragged street urchins were making a peddler's life hell as he tried to coax his old swayback nag on down the street amid other weary and sleepy-eyed beggars, clerks, and shopkeepers. All were starting out a new day. Gabe looked up anxiously as the coach made a sharp turn and passed under the archway into the Admiralty courtyard. Gabe's knuckles turned white from grasping the window handle as the coach's wheels slipped on the dew-wet cobblestones and then came to a sudden halt in front of the Admiralty's main entrance. Anthony smiled at Gabe's obvious fright, wondering what he was thinking as he visited the Admiralty for the first time.

A doorman opened the coach as soon as it stopped. He looked puzzled when his gaze first fell upon a midshipman. With the arrival of a crested private coach, the man was expecting more than a mere boy. He looked somewhat relieved when he searched further and saw Captain Anthony.

"This way, my Lord," the doorman said.

Anthony still hadn't gotten used to the title. "Lord Anthony" had always meant his father. As the two followed the messenger up the steps and into the spacious entrance hall, Anthony could see Gabe was overcome with awe.

His first visit, Anthony thought again. *If luck serves Gabe well, there will be many visits, all pleasant.*

Out of nowhere a clerk appeared. He obviously knew Captain Anthony and had been on the lookout for him. "If you would be so kind as to wait in here, my Lord. His Lordship knows you're here. He's finishing up a complicated matter and assures me he will be with you directly."

The messenger turned to leave, and then paused in his stride, saying, "I'm sorry to hear about your father, my Lord. He was a good man, a good leader. If circumstances had been different, many believe he would have been First Lord."

Gil nodded, "It's good of you to remember."

As the messenger left the small room, Anthony approached the small fireplace to warm his stiff and aching bones. As they waited, it dawned on Anthony that he and Gabe were waiting in one of the small private anterooms, not in one of the larger rooms that would be filled with unemployed half-pay captains, commanders and lieutenants, all looking for a berth or a command.

Anthony turned to Gabe, who had thus far said nothing. Gabe was staring out of the only window in the room. The cold February wind whipped against the windowpanes, and Gabe spoke.

"Wind's picking up, temperature's dropping, and it's cloudy. It'll probably snow tonight. Father would say 'a night not fit for neither man nor beast, and certainly not fit for a sailor.'"

Anthony and Gabe smiled, thinking of their father's words. At that time, the messenger returned, "The First Lord will see you now, Lord Anthony."

He hesitated, not wanting to offend Anthony, and then found the right words. "Perhaps the young gentleman would like to take a turn through the halls, sir." It was the messenger's polite way of saying the room was needed for someone more important than a midshipman.

"I'll wait outside with Dagan," Gabe volunteered.

Anthony had forgotten Dagan, who had been sitting atop the coach with the driver. No doubt they had found a warm spot, if not a touch of something to warm their insides.

***

LORD SANDWICH WAS STARING out the window as Anthony entered. "Gil -- Lord Anthony, I should say. How are you?"

The two shook hands as old friends. Anthony had played cards with the First Lord on many occasions. He had also dined with him and his mistress here at the Admiralty. For a while Anthony had been a member, along with the First Lord, at the infamous Hellfire Club. Anthony knew that without Sandwich's influence, the Navy would be in worse shape than it was. Many blamed Sandwich, but in fact the Prime Minister, Lord North, was responsible for most of the Navy's shortcomings.

Leaving off the title, Sandwich said, "Ah Gil, Parliament is in love with you, my boy. Having saved the Honest John Convoy from those cutthroats has made you England's darling for the time being. Front page of *The Gazette*, no less. But the truth be known, the reason for such a display of admiration as you received, is because you saved a good many from financial ruin. That includes several members of Parliament, not the least of which is your brother-in-law. It was through his insistence that you were knighted so quickly, not only to honor you, but also something to make your father proud in his last days. By the by, the Prince sends his regrets about your being herded through his Majesty's court so fast. He would like some time to visit with you, once our business is complete. Speaking of business, have you taken care of your father's affairs?"

"Yes," Anthony answered.

"You've met your brother?" inquired the First Lord. Anthony nodded. "He has the makings of a fine officer," continued Lord Sandwich. "But watch out for him. Some will try, and may even succeed, in using him against you."

Taken aback, Anthony, somewhat roused,

asked, "In what way?"

"In many ways! Wherever there's envy or jealously, wherever there is an insult, real or imagined, people will try to hurt you through any means possible. Just be on guard, Lord Anthony. Be on guard."

"Aye, sir."

"Now for the business at hand. For several years now, grievances by the colonies have mounted. Most feel it's only a time before verbal conflicts turn into open hostilities and war. There is growing concern in the House of Commons as to whether the Navy can maintain control of the seas if war does break out. It is most certain France, and maybe even Spain, will enter along with the colonies. You know how thin we are stretched now. War could be devastating. Right now pirates, who many in Parliament feel are in cahoots with the Colonials, are wreaking havoc on our merchant ships.

"This is not to mention the damned blackguards who have allegiance to no country. These damned pirates are a menace. They prey upon the trade lanes in the Caribbean and off the American coast with seeming impunity. Your recent success has made you the ideal person to deal with this problem. Yours will be an independent command. You will have leeway to deal with this threat as you see fit. You are to assume command of *Drakkar,* a forty-four. She has a near full complement and should be completing all preparations to put to sea. Her former captain has decided to retire rather than face hostilities with the colonies. The *Drakkar* already has a full slate of officers, but I'm sure you'll want Lieutenant Buck and a few others. Just leave a list of names with my secretary, and he'll see to it."

"When do you expect me to sail?" Anthony asked.

"Within a fortnight."

"And where are we bound, sir?"

"English Harbour, Antigua."

Chapter Three

BEFORE REPORTING TO *HMS Drakkar*, Anthony had taken the time to visit Deerfield. He wanted to see his mother before getting underway for another commission, one that might take years. Gabe had been sent on to the ship. Mother would only have to see Gabe and she would know who his father was. That would only cause a stir and Anthony wasn't ready to deal with that so soon after his father's passing.

Looking back, the trip had served to depress Anthony more than cheer him. Deerfield was in fine order but his mother had been sick the entire time he was at home. She seemed to be in a fog or confused state. She constantly repeated things she'd just said, all the while asking Anthony, did he know when his father would return home? She refused to acknowledge that Lord Anthony was dead.

These thoughts were still on Anthony's mind as he hired a small boat to take him out to *Drakkar*. His exact time to arrive had not been set, and therefore his gig would not be awaiting his arrival. A brisk southwesterly breeze filled the main sail. The dip of the boat's bow on choppy waves created a constant salt spray. The old man and his grandson appeared to be oblivious, but the spindrift had Anthony constantly wiping his face. Anthony's cox'n, Bart, and his servant, Silas, had draped a tarpaulin over Anthony's sea chest and themselves to keep them dry and protect them.

As the boat pushed through the chilly harbour's water, Anthony glanced at the maimed old sailor at the tiller. His hands were gnarled and rheumatoid. A single crutch lay beside the tiller, bringing attention to the man's peg leg.

The old man must have sensed Anthony's gaze and offered, "Name's Pilcher, sir, former gunner on the *Hawke*. Lost me timber at Cape Finisterre, I did."

Anthony nodded and could only guess at how many such men had given so much only to be discharged and left to fend for themselves. These veterans were used up, and then cast aside like the hulks of old rotting ships. Nobody remembered their sacrifices. Lost in his thoughts, it took Pilcher's cry, "There she be, Cap'n," to break his reverie.

Drakkar – Dragon. Would her cannon breathe fire upon England's enemies as her mythical namesake had done? Someone had spent a great amount of time and care carving the figurehead. No small sum was spent on just the gold leaf. As the wind picked up, Anthony could see *Drakkar's* copper as she strained at her cable. He likened her to a racehorse ready to be off. Much to the boatman's despair, Anthony had him circle the ship – his ship. Like the figurehead, the stern-gallery was done with great care. *How long will she remain so ornate,* Anthony wondered? *Ah, she is the picture of perfection. She'd be even more beautiful with all her sails set and running before the wind.*

"Lovely ain't she, Cap'n? Just as lovely as a virgin on 'er wedding night," Bart volunteered.

Closer now, Anthony could hear and make out the activity aboard his new ship. Aft by the entry port, Lieutenant Dunn had his marines turned out. The crew was being made ready for his arrival, and God help the man that caused embarrassment to the First Lieutenant, Mr. Buck, with the captain coming aboard.

"Boat approaching," declared a sentry.

"Very well," acknowledged the first lieutenant.

"Boat ahoy!" The challenge rang out.

"*Drakkar!*"

The challenge had been given and the boatman's response left no doubt that the man coming aboard would be second only to God in controlling their lives in the foreseeable future.

Anthony removed his boat cloak and tossed it to his cox'n, Bart. No need in getting tangled and tossing one's own self arsehole over elbows in front of the entire crew. Anthony timed the swell just right, and it was little more than a step from the little boat to *Drakkar's* battens and a pull on the man ropes through the entry port. No sooner had his head appeared above the entry port than honors began. The sudden noise from the pipers and the slap of muskets from the marines presenting arms was almost deafening as all cadences blended together to announce the arrival of their captain. As he cleared the entry port and stepped on deck, Anthony paused momentarily; just a moment to fully enjoy the honors he was being rendered. In that brief period, he glanced about the ship, taking it all in. Her tall, tapering mast, every rope, block and tackle, the polished brass and furled sails. The assembled crew and blackened guns. She was a frigate all right. A damned big frigate to be sure, but a frigate all the same. Anthony could smell the tar, the faint odor of gun oil and the sea. Yes, *Drakkar* was ready, and God help him, so was he. Anthony felt like he was home.

"Ah, Mr. Buck!" Anthony said as the first lieutenant greeted him. "You've done a fine job, as usual."

"Thank you, sir. Bart and Silas are seeing that your things get stowed below. You've much more room than on the *Recourse*," Buck told Anthony.

"As have you, I hope," answered Anthony with a smile. "Now if you will be so kind as to muster the crew aft."

"Aye, sir," Buck replied, and then turning to the bosun, he repeated the order.

Reaching into his pocket for his orders, Anthony felt his father's old pipe. A chill went through him. It was like he could feel his father's presence. He then pulled out his orders and with a firm voice read them to the ship's company.

"By the Commissioner for executing the office of Lord High Admiral...To Captain Lord Gilbert Anthony...His Majesty's Frigate *Drakkar*...willing and requiring you forthwith to go on board and take upon you the charge and command of captain..."

After his reading in, Anthony turned to his first lieutenant, "Dismiss the crew and then come to my cabin, Mr. Buck."

"I'll be there directly, Captain."

***

BART AND SILAS WERE unpacking their captain's belongings when Anthony entered the cabin. Bart was Anthony's cox'n. The two had been together since Bart was a seaman and Anthony a young lieutenant. Silas? Silas was many things – servant, secretary and coffee maker extraordinaire. His coffee was legendary. It was rare when a visitor who had had the pleasure of a cup of Silas's coffee didn't request more on a subsequent visit.

While no place on a crowded ship could be considered private, the captain's quarters were as close as it came. Anthony gazed at the stern windows. They crossed the entire length of his quarters. He looked closely at the handiwork of the craftsman where timbers had been fitted after the ship had been razed. They had done a remarkable job.

Drakkar was considered a fifth rate forty-four gun frigate. However, she was originally launched as a French sixty-four, a third rate. She had been taken by Hawke's squadron as they defeated the French fleet at Quibron Bay in 1759. She was now one of King George's largest frigates, still carrying the twenty-four pounders that were her main armament when she was a sixty-four. A broadside from *Drakkar* would be devastating.

It was getting dark and as the sun went down so did the temperature. The cabin would be damp and cold in Portsmouth Harbour. However, a week in the tropics should not only help the cold, but also the ache in Anthony's bones. He looked at the two ornamental partitions left by the previous captain. They hid his sleeping cabin and the chart room. The man had also left his table, chairs, a mahogany wardrobe and desk. All were of good quality and had to have been expensive. Anthony couldn't help but wonder if his predecessor was extremely wealthy or just in an extreme hurry. Either way, he was thankful for the furnishings that had been left aboard.

The marine sentry announced Buck's arrival, "First Lieutenant, zur." Buck entered and nodded his greeting to Bart and Silas.

"Well, Rupert, what do you think of her?" Anthony asked.

"To tell you the truth, sir, I'm in love. She's a big one all right, nigh on to 1,300 tons, but she'll sail as well as any keel-laid 38. I figure she'll out-sail anything she can't out gun."

"What about the crew?" Anthony asked.

"We got two-hundred ninety-six aboard now. That's twenty-four short, but the port admiral said he'd have us another two dozen before we sail. Probably clear out the prison hulks and such. However, we're fortunate in our warrants. True professionals they are. Even the purser. He can count, knows his weights, and seems more honest than most of his kind. Ole Peckham, the master off of *Recourse,* has reported. I know you asked for him. The bosun is big, burly, and Irish, God help us. He is a little too free with his start-er to suit me, but he'll learn my ways before too long. As for the young gentlemen, we have a full load. Most are ripe and bursting at the seams to make captain."

This brought a chuckle from Anthony.

"Gabe, your brother, is senior," Buck continued. "He seems to have settled in well enough already. We got an admiral's nephew on board. His name is Frances Markham. He and Gabe seem to have hit it off well enough."

Buck then took a breath and expelled a sigh. "Your brother-in-law, however, has sent us a little shit that could pass for a drowned rat along with a letter. I, ah, took the liberty of reading it since it wasn't sealed or addressed to you private-ly."

Anthony nodded.

"Seems the little fellow's father was killed sudden-like. So, as to help the boy's mother out, the local squire used his influence with Hugh to help the young gentleman get a berth. Probably to get him outta the way, so to speak. All buxoms and smiles, I'm told!"

Anthony glared at Buck and exclaimed, "The young gentleman?"

"Ere, uh, no sir, Captain. The lad's mother, the one the squire is bent on helping out."

This made Anthony chuckle. "We've heard that story before, I believe, Rupert."

"Aye, I believe we have," Buck replied.

***

"Cap'n? It's time, Cap'n. Here's ye a cup of coffee jes like ye like it. Silas is getting some hot water for yer shave."

Anthony raised himself and grunted his thanks to Bart. The coffee was scalding hot, so he took a careful sip. This helped to wash away some of the leftover taste of cigars and brandy. It had been a tradition with Anthony since his first command to invite all the officers, warrants, and midshipmen to dine their first night underway. It was a good way to learn about each of them. It was amazing what a captain could elicit from his officers after a good meal and a glass or two of wine. Often the captain would discover strengths and weaknesses that might otherwise take weeks to discern. One frequently spied the petty tyrants, the snobs, etc. It was a trick his father had passed on to him. A second sip of coffee and Anthony realized Bart was in mid-sentence and he hadn't heard the first of it.

"What's that?" he asked Bart.

The cox'n eyed his captain. "More-n-usual with the spirits, Cap'n?"

"Hush! Damn your ugly eyes," Anthony snarled.

"Huh!" snorted Bart. "I were telling ye the master, Mr. Peckham, said it was to be unseasonably warm today and we's headed in the right general direction with a fair wind."

Anthony couldn't help but laugh even though it caused his head to hurt. "Right general direction." That sounded like old Peckham, but God help the man who didn't steer the course the master set.

Silas entered, "It'll be light soon, Cap'n. Here's yer breakfast and Mr. Buck would like to see ye soon as convenient, sir."

"Very well. Have the sentry pass the word for Mr. Buck to lay to my cabin, and we'll have a cup of coffee together."

"Aye, sir," Silas replied then departed.

Anthony could tell something was amiss as soon as Buck entered the cabin. "Sit down, sir. You look ready to explode."

"Aye, Captain. It's the fourth lieutenant, Mr. Witzenfeld, sir. He's already placed a petty officer on report for disrespect."

"How so?" Anthony questioned.

"Mr. Witz, that's what they call Witzenfeld, sir. Well, we had just called all hands to shorten sail. Mr. Witz tells a new hand, a landsman, to lend a hand and clew up the sails. Well, sir, the poor sod was dumbfounded and just stood there gawkish like. That set Mr. Witz off. He started cussing and screaming at the man telling him to obey his orders or feel the cat. Avery, one of the bosun's mates, attempted to explain what was wrong but then Witz jumped on him, berating him as the son of a worthless whore. He said, "When I give an order, it's to be carried out by the person I gave it to." By that time, most of the crew had gathered. Avery had had enough of Witz's name calling and said to Witz, "'E's a bloody landsman, sir, can't ye tell? 'E ain't got no fooking idea what clew up means. Mr. Witz then promised Avery a dozen lashes for his disrespect and insolence."

Anthony shook his head upon hearing Buck's tale. "A bad beginning."

"Aye, Captain, a bad one all right."

Suddenly a shrill scream broke the momentary silence. It was more like that of a child than a man. In a bound, Anthony and Buck were through the cabin door and up on deck. Dagan had a hold of Mr. Davy, the young midshipman the squire had made arrangements for. The lad was twisting, thrashing, and trying his best to get to the fourth lieutenant, Mr. Witzenfeld. However, it was Gabe who stood in front of the young boy, face to face with Witzenfeld. Dagan was speaking in a soothing fashion to calm and quiet the angry lad. Mr. Witzenfeld was touching a bloody lip. As he withdrew his hand from his mouth it went to the hilt of his sword, and he took a threatening step forward toward the young midshipman. Gabe was there, but it was Dagan who, releasing Mr. Davy, took a sudden step forward. His cold black eyes seemed to penetrate, and Witz's body gave a sudden involuntary shudder. Mr. Witz stopped dead in his tracks, his skin turning pale as moisture broke out across his freckled forehead.

"Mr. Witzenfeld! To your cabin, sir," Anthony ordered. He then turned to Gabe, "Mr. Anthony, see that Mr. Davy gets cleaned up and brought to my cabin forthwith."

"Aye, aye, sir," Gabe answered.

"Bart!"

"Here, Cap'n."

"Follow me."

"Aye, Cap'n."

"Mr. Buck, you have the ship."

"Aye, aye, sir."

In the privacy of his quarters, Anthony turned to Bart. "Go talk with Dagan and maybe the master, Mr. Peckham. I saw him on deck. Talk with them in private, but get me their side of what just happened on deck."

Bart nodded. As he was leaving, Anthony said, "Damme, but this is a bad beginning." Bart paused just inside the cabin door. He looked at

Anthony and said, "Aye, Cap'n, but sometimes it's best to get rid of a bad apple afore it spoils the whole barrel."

"Bad apple!" Anthony exclaimed. "Damn your eyes, you're talking about a King's officer."

Bart replied, "Bad apples come in all forms, sir!" Then he was out the door. *Damn him*, Anthony thought. For ten years, the cox'n always seemed to get the last word.

At that time, the marine sentry announced, "Mr. Anthony, zur."

When Gabe entered, Anthony asked, "Where's Mr. Davy?"

"With the surgeon, sir."

"Was he hurt?"

"Not outwardly, sir."

Anthony shook his head, "By outwardly you mean he's hurting inside, as in his heart?"

"And his pride," Gabe replied.

"I see," said Anthony to his brother, suddenly wondering if his insight may have come from experience.

"I thought," Gabe began, "that if we could talk maybe we wouldn't have to put Mr. Davy through that ordeal again." It was then that Anthony realized that Gabe was still standing at attention.

"Relax, Gabe, there's no one here but us. Have a seat and tell me what happened."

"Well, sir, you know the lad's father was killed just recently. A hunting accident, I'm told. Mistaken for a deer by the squire's overseer."

This caused Anthony to raise his eyebrows. "I hadn't heard that. Only that he'd died suddenly of an accident."

"Well," Gabe continued, "Since the ah – accident, the squire's been paying particular interest to the lad's mother."

"A very handsome lass, I'm told," Anthony said, recalling Buck's description. "All buxom and smiles."

"Yes sir, I've been told the same," Gabe replied as he continued his story. "The boy was sent off to sea quick as you please. Anyway, Witz knew about the ah... arrangement. He's a cruel person, sir. He asked Mr. Davy in a smirking manner if he was warm enough last night. He went on to say he shouldn't worry any about his mother cause he was sure the squire had her all tucked in nice and warm. Well, it dawned on Mr. Davy what Witz was talking about. He then told Witz he had a vulgar mouth, and he'd better shut it, or he'd call him out."

"He's got nerve, the lad has," Anthony responded.

"Aye, sir," replied Gabe. "Well, Witz then called him a snot-nosed little shit who didn't know his arsehole from a hawse-hole. He told Davy he should be damn glad the squire considered his mother a nice enough piece of mutton that he'd go to the trouble of packing her brat off so's he could enjoy her pleasures. Witz then told Davy if he didn't mind his betters, he'd personally see his arse put on the beach, and his mother would be turned out and have to peddle her wares with all the other common trollops." Gabe gave a deep sigh. "The little bugger was fighting mad, he was. He set to have it out right then and there. He told Witz he was a filthy-minded person who was so obscene he didn't deserve to wear the King's coat. He went on to say that if Witz ever spoke so rudely about his mother again, he'd kill him. Witz then laughed at the boy and shoved him. When he did, Davy retaliated by slapping Witz in the face and bloodying his lip."

"So Lieutenant Witzenfeld laid hands on Davy first?" Anthony asked.

"Aye, sir. Several witnesses saw it."

Anthony told Gabe he appreciated what he had done for Mr. Davy, standing up for the young boy as he had. He then sent Gabe to fetch the first lieutenant.

On his way out, Gabe turned back to Anthony and stated, "By the by, sir, I knew Witz from the Revenue Cutter *Raven*. We were both mids then."

"Well, there it be, Cap'n - as bad an apple as ye can have!" Bart had returned with much the same story from Dagan and the master as had been told by Gabe.

When Buck arrived, Anthony retold the story, leaving out little.

"Same as I hear from gunner Williams," Buck related. "Do you want me to talk to Witz, Captain?"

"No, I'll do it. But for this last incident involving Mr. Davy, I thought I'd do something trivial to show support for my officer without hurting a good man. But now, the crew has to know they can trust me, and that I'll not allow them to be abused by a petty tyrant. While we're talking, Rupert, it's also important for the officers to know that just because Gabe's my brother he's not to be given special treatment. He's to be treated as any other midshipman. In truth, I don't think he expects or wishes any special treatment. If anything, I will be harder because of father's expectations," Anthony said as he recalled his father's words – *I taught you well enough, I'd like you to teach him.*

Buck could feel the burden his captain was carrying, "Young Gabe will be fine, sir, but to tell the truth, I don't trust Lieutenant Witzenfeld. I'd as soon cast the whoreson adrift in a lifeboat with a loaded pistol and a pint of water."

Anthony couldn't help but laugh at Buck's recommendation.

"No. Put a good master's mate on watch with him with specific instructions on calling you should the need arise. Now, if you will, send Witz down to see me."

As Buck left, Bart said, "Ain't a bad idea he had, sir."

Just then the marine announced, "Fourth Lieutenant, zur." *The sentry is getting a workout today,* Anthony thought.

Anthony had Witzenfeld relate his side of the story for both incidents, first involving Avery, then Mr. Davy.

When the man had finished, Anthony began. "First, let's discuss your error in handling Avery and the landsman. As an officer, I expect you to know the abilities of each man in your division. We've tried to spread out the landsmen so no watch would have more than its fair share. Since we are all new to each other, I'd expect you to trust your petty officers. When you see one trying to step in or teach a man, you should back off and let the petty officer do his job. By doing so, you'll find the men appreciate you more and will strive harder to please you. Now, as I've said, we are all new to each other, therefore, we'll chalk it up to one big misunderstanding. We'll have a new beginning. We'll hold Avery's rum ration. Therefore, it will be seen as I'm supporting you."

Before Anthony could finish his sentence, Lieutenant Witzenfeld seem to go into a fit. He shouted, "Hold his rum ration! Sir, I ordered him flogged -- a dozen at least."

Witz's outburst turned Anthony livid. He had been sitting, but now he stood abruptly, and slammed his fist on his desk, knocking over a half-filled cup of coffee. "Who the hell do you think you are to order anything? My God! Have you forgotten that I command this ship? Damme sir, have you not heard a word I've said?" Anthony paused to gain control of his emotions.

"Another thing, sir. Don't ever let me hear of you making disparaging comments to anyone as you have done to Mr. Davy. If he were older, I'm sure he would have called you out. Furthermore, I'm not so sure I would have intervened."

"Why should you, sir?" commented Witz with somewhat of a smirk on his face. "I'd enjoy the exercise."

"Damn you to hell, man!" said Anthony in a fit of rage. "You go too far, sir. You try me. Do you not have a heart? No compassion? Damn you and your insolence! How would you care to taste the cat?"

Witz must have realized he'd gone too far. He was visibly shaken at the threat of the cat. "But, sir, I'm an officer."

"Then act like one! Now get out of my quarters."

Witz fairly ran out of the cabin.

"Here, Cap'n." Anthony turned to see Silas standing there with a fresh cup of coffee. "A splash 'o something to settle yer humors, sir."

Anthony took a drink of the warm, dark liquid and almost choked...a splash indeed! Silas had given him a warm cup of coffee flavored brandy.

Chapter Four

As *Drakkar* made her way through the Channel she was rocked by a blustering gale. Waves swept over the bow and sluiced down the scuppers carrying anybody and anything not secured with it. Sails filled with wind one moment would go slack, and then with a thunderous pop fill again from winds so perverse the master would shake his head in disbelief. The burly bosun McMorgan's voice could constantly be heard as he coaxed the men to their duties by either blistering them with his tongue or a thrash from his rope starter.

While life for the crew was hell, it was not much better for those in the midshipmen's berth. For Davy and Gabe it was worse. Davy had unfortunately wound up in Lieutenant Witzenfield's division.

Witzenfield was clever enough to make life so miserable that young Davy confided in Gabe that death seemed more attractive than life.

All the guns had new lashings. With the constant roll of the ship from the gale, a strain was placed on the ropes and they stretched. Seeing loose lashings, Witz ordered Davy to take up the slack on all the twenty-four pounders in his section. A bruised, beaten, and silent Davy made his way to his mess after completing his task.

"Damme sir, but what has happened to your face?" Markham asked.

Davy had slipped and butted his face on one of the big cannons. His lips were battered and bloody. Tasting the wine Markham offered made him wince, but soon Davy felt warm and the pain seemed to lessen.

Miller, the normally foul-tempered ex-topman who now served the midshipmen showed a gentle side as he used a wet rag to wipe away the blood from the young gentleman's face and lips. "Ought t' see th' surgeon to my way o' thinking. You could get festers if ye lips ain't treated proper like."

At that time, Gabe entered the mess. He was wet, cold and tired after standing his watch. However, seeing Davy's face and hearing the story behind it caused him to grow angry. "That son of a bitch. Given half a chance I'd run him through."

"Aye," Markham agreed. "Maybe we should request to speak to Mr. Buck about it."

Calming down some, Gabe replied, "No, officially we've got no complaint. People get injured going about ship's work all the time."

"Who's injured?"

As the three turned it was a smirking Lieutenant Witzenfield who stood before them. "Who's injured I asked?"

"Mr. Davy," Markham answered, not wanting Gabe to say something he'd be sorry for.

Taking another step into the berth Witzenfield ducked his head to avoid an overhead beam. "Come here boy. Do you need to see the surgeon?"

"No, sir," Davy answered.

"I see. Are you fit for duty?"

"Yes, sir."

"Do you recall my orders to secure the lashings on my cannons?"

"Yes, sir. I was securing them when I fell against one injuring my face," Davy muttered through his battered lips.

"Huh! Aren't you the King's hard bargain? I've just checked and every one of the lashings was loose as a fiddler's bitch. I think an hour or two at the masthead should make you more conscientious when you next carry out a task."

Unable to remain quiet any longer Gabe spoke out, "But sir, the ropes are new. They'll stretch again in a couple of hours if this gale keeps up."

"Ahum! You may very well be right, Mr. Anthony. I should have thought of that. However, never to steal one's thunder, you can wake Mr. Davy every two hours so that he can make sure the lashings are secure."

"Damn you!" Davy blurted as Witz was leaving the berth.

Wheeling around, Witz glared. "What was that?"

Gabe and Markham were too shocked to reply.

45

Miller, the old salt, used his savvy in responding to the officer, "The young sir said thank you. Only 'is lips are so busted it be hard to understand. 'E can barely speak as yer ownself can see." All the time Miller was patting Davy on the head and shoulders. "It's a bad time 'e be havin' of it, sir."

Realizing he'd get nowhere with pursuing it, Witz snarled, "One day you'll make a mistake and I'll be there. Mark my word, one day."

As soon as he'd dressed and shaved, Kramer, the surgeon, made his way to the wardroom for breakfast. Settling into his usual spot he spied Lieutenant Witzenfield.

Seeing Witz reminded him of young Davy, whose blisters became sores, sores that became scabs only to be torn off and became sores again. His injured lips were so battered it was days before he could eat anything but gruel. Now in his third day of being awakened every two hours to check gun lashings, he had a croup. But the torture was not only directed at Davy but at Mr. Anthony as well. How many times had he been mast-headed? He'd been given three lots of extra duty in three days. How many times had he been sent aloft to check the splices where something had been repaired? These tasks were usually given after dark or during a gale. All this time the captain stayed silent. Kramer could only guess at his patience. How much longer would it be before Davy or Gabe broke? Kramer had seen Gabe in a quiet but heated conversation with Dagan.

Was Witz so stupid he couldn't sense the stares he was getting from the man? How long before Dagan threw caution to the wind and took justice into his own hands? Gabe couldn't control him forever, not with Witz treating Gabe so cruelly. Kramer couldn't help but think a lot of Davy's abuse by Witz was to get at Gabe, to make him cross that line.

With as sharp a look as he could muster, Kramer tried to demonstrate all the resentment he felt as he spoke to the wardroom as a whole.

"It appears our esteemed fourth lieutenant has single-handedly taken upon himself all these duties normally carried out by the bosun, the master-at-arms, the first lieutenant and at times even almighty God himself!"

Peckham, the master, Marine Lieutenant Dunn, Lieutenant Earl and Lieutenant Pitts all looked astonished as the surgeon spoke.

"Tell me, sir," Kramer was again speaking, this time directly to Witz, "Do you have a grievance against Mr. Anthony and Mr. Davy?"

Shocked that he was being addressed so, Witz replied, "Why would I have a grievance?"

"Your actions, sir. Anybody not totally blind can see you have an agenda."

"I resent your accusations," Witz replied, his anger starting to show, "I'm merely doing my duty to make good officers of them, unlike some lickspittles."

Standing, Lieutenant Earl spoke, "To whom

are you addressing as lickspittle?"

Witz knew he was now in jeopardy as both lieutenants were his senior. He also knew that while he outranked the surgeon and the master, he'd best tread lightly with both. "Oh, not officers," he replied. "I just want to do my part to make better seamen and officers out of them, as I stated."

***

"Huh!" Peckham snorted. "You'd do well to have Mr. Anthony help you with your navigation."

"There's nothing wrong with my navigation," Witz hurled back.

"Nothing wrong...Well, damme, my boy, but where's the black ivory?"

"Black ivory?"

"Why yes, by your noon readings yesterday, *Drakkar* should be slap dab in the middle of Africa, by God!" This caused a howl from the rest of the officers.

Scowling at the master, Witz almost screamed, "You lie, dammit, tell them now, you lie."

"Careful sir," Lieutenant Dunn addressed Witz.

"He can't talk to me that way," Witz cried.

"What you gonna do boy, masthead me?" Peckham responded.

Trying to allay the situation, Lieutenant Pitts spoke quietly, "Let's all calm down." Being next to Witz, he placed his hand on his shoulder and continued, "It wasn't long ago I felt I had to prove myself. I realize now I already have. I made lieutenant. And with good luck I'll make captain and then admiral."

This created another howl as Pitts knew it would but at least the situation had been diffused. Later when Witz relieved Pitts on watch, Pitts offered some more advice. "I don't know what you have against Mr. Anthony and it's none of my business. But just because the cap'n hasn't said anything don't mean he isn't watching and so's Mr. Buck. I'd not cross Mr. Buck if I was you. He's got a mean streak for those he doesn't like."

"I'm not concerned about Buck or the cap'n," Witz snorted. "Captain or not he has to do his duty regardless of family."

"It's your career," Pitts answered, turning to go down to his cabin. As he turned he saw Dagan. He had to have heard the conversation. Well, Witz had been warned by all, now his actions were his own worry. Pitts was ready for a glass of wine and three hours of sleep.

***

IT HAD BEEN FIFTEEN days since they had slipped moorings at Portsmouth. Anthony had not spoken to Witz since that first day underway. On the surface, everything appeared fine. Appeared, he thought to himself. He wasn't blind; he'd been mindful of Witzenfeld's actions and treatment of Gabe and Davy. How many times had he seen Buck looking at him, just a nod and Buck would have made Witz's life hell? How many times had Bart said something? Even Silas, the silent one, said, "Mr. Anthony's bound to break sooner or later, sir."

Anthony glanced down at his log. It was full of entries, but how could a few lines describe all that went on? A sailor would know, but never a landsman. Fifteen days-but it seemed longer. They had dealt with heavy seas, gales, and strong head winds. Then for a whole day they lay be-calmed.

It was all hands to shorten sails, then set more sails, and then reef down. It seemed every evolution was carried out a hundred times. But it all served a purpose. The ship was coming togeth-er. All except Witz. Command was a solemn duty at times. Anthony could recall the longing for command he'd experienced as a lieutenant. But as Lord Sandwich had warned, "Command was doing one's duty, not what one wished to do." He knew he had to address the Witz situation soon.

Thinking of Buck, Anthony had to give him credit for a fine job with the crew. He was not completely satisfied with gun drill, but even that was improving.

"Cleared for action in ten minutes and fifteen seconds," Buck had said snapping his watch shut.

Yes, that was far better than the fourteen minutes plus on their first drill – but not good enough. Fire drill was still dismal. That had to im-prove. Anthony also sensed camaraderie building among the officers. He commented on his observations to Buck one evening.

"Yes, sir," Buck agreed. "Did you know young Gabe can sing, sir?"

Anthony didn't.

"He and Mr. Earl, the second lieutenant, will get together after their watch-weather permitting-and put on a fair show. The crew seems to enjoy it. Mr. Earl has a flute, and Gabe has some sort of little stringed instrument. When they get to going on a real sassy tune, sir, half the damn crew will dance up a jig. You should come hear it, sir."

"Maybe, I will," replied Anthony.

"By the by, sir, Mr. Gabe has the makings of a fine officer. He'll do you proud, sir. I'm certain."

"Well, thank you, Rupert. I'm glad to hear it. Your evaluation means a great deal to me."

***

HEARING THE MUSIC AND merriment through the open skylight, Anthony strolled on deck. He saw the master's mate nudge the officer of the watch.

Mr. Pitts turned and greeted his captain. "Evening sir. We're sou'sou'west and about to take in another reef. The master promises a hot night and hotter morrow."

"Mr. Peckham is usually right. Are you enjoying the festivities?" Anthony asked his third lieutenant.

"Yes, sir. I don't have an ear for music like

some, but it makes the watch go quicker to have something going on. I've stressed to the lookouts to keep close vigil."

Anthony was glad to hear Pitts say this. He was also mad with himself for not thinking the activities on the fo'c'sle could possibly distract the lookouts from their duties. This was something to consider.

Lieutenant Pitts had returned to the wheel and made a show of checking the compass. Anthony knew this was to give him his space on the quarterdeck. As Anthony turned, he spied Dagan lounging against the bulwark amidships, puffing on his pipe. Anthony approached the man wanting to get to know "Gabe's uncle and protector" better.

"I say, Dagan, I didn't know you smoked a pipe."

"Aye, sir, mostly at night when I have the time to fill the bowl and enjoy it full. I can't abide lighting up, having it go out, and then fetching another match."

"I see," said Anthony. "I have my father's old pipe and I intend to see if I like it better than cigars."

"I have some fine tobacco," Dagan volunteered. "Blended for your father by his tobacconist. He always got me a tin when he ordered his."

"Why thank you," Anthony said. Not wanting to end his conversation, Anthony volunteered, "The master assures us it'll be a hot day tomorrow."

Dagan took his pipe from his mouth and looked at Anthony with cold hard eyes. "Storm on the horizon."

"Storms!" rebuked Anthony. "The master's rarely wrong about the weather, Dagan."

"More 'n one kind of storm, Cap'n. You've been told." He was then gone like a ghost. Anthony felt like a midshipman who'd just been dismissed by his betters. *Storms*!

***

THE DAY WAS AS hot as the master predicted. A gentle wind blew sou'westerly, but did little to reduce the heat. After a good breakfast and shave, Anthony went on deck with Bart trailing.

"Ah, Mr. Buck! I hope you've broken your fast."

"Aye, Captain," Buck replied.

"Well," said Anthony, "I believe this would be an opportune time for gun drill. Beat to quarters if you will, and clear for action."

"Directly, sir." Buck answered and gave the order. He had already taken out his watch.

"Bart!"

"Aye, Cap'n!"

"See the purser if you will. Give him my respects, and tell him I'd take it kindly if he were to donate those barrels that had contained rancid meat for target practice. They should make fair targets for our gunners."

As Bart turned to go, Anthony saw he was grinning.

"Bart!"

"Aye, sir!"

"What pray tell has humored you so to produce such a grin?"

"I was just imagining what kind of lie the purser would make up to explain the loss of the barrels. No doubt it'll cover not only the barrels but that beef that we fed to the sharks."

"Think so, do you?" Anthony asked, seeing the humor in Bart's prediction.

"No doubt, sir, and in such a way so as to shirk the blame and still show as much profit as plausible for himself." Bart had the purser pegged right enough.

No sooner had the order "clear for action" been given than the ship became a beehive of activity. The drummer started his roll. The below watch came up on deck with wild cries of encouragement from the petty officers. It was like a mad dash as the crew flung themselves to their tasks.

Bulkheads were removed-with care, Anthony hoped, thinking of the ornamental partitions in his cabin. The decks were drenched with seawater, and then sand was strewn. Breathless powder monkeys ran with their arms weighted down with cartridges for the guns. Fire parties took their places. The marines under Lieutenant Dunn smartly made their way to their battle stations. The surgeon and his mates had made their wares ready. The gun crews cast off lashings and removed covers from the breeches. Then with a strain, they tugged at the tackles to drag the heavy guns inboard to be loaded. Powder and shot were rammed home. The muzzles were then depressed. Once again, the crews tugged like demons at the tackles. The guns were run out through open ports. The sweat-drenched men then stood back signifying they were ready.

Anthony sensed Buck approaching.

"Cleared for action, sir-nine minutes flat," Buck said proudly.

"Excellent, Mr. Buck, excellent. Now let's check for their accuracy. Please be certain they know to aim at the barrels and not the boat crews."

"No fear, Captain. The purser is in his hole, not in the jolly boat." Buck had not been able to contain his own little jab at the purser.

Hearing the snickers from the gun crew who had overheard Buck's comment, Anthony re-buked Buck good-naturedly. "Mr. Buck, kindly watch your remarks, sir. Mr. Lott holds a king's warrant."

"And lots more 'e does when given the chance, sir," some unknown voice within the crowd quipped, making fun of the purser's name.

"Silence," Buck ordered, but doing so with a smile. *It is good when men can laugh so*, Anthony thought. Laughter usually meant a contented crew.

***

"MASTER-AT-ARMS, PASS THE WORD for the mas-ter-at-arms to report aft to Mr. Witzenfeld in the great cabin!" Anthony looked at Buck, who exclaimed, "Jesus wept. By gawd, I'll string up the sniveling shit before sundown."

As Buck's head disappeared below the companionway on his way to the captain's quarters, Anthony was filled with a sudden urge to follow and see first hand what was going on, even though his better judgment told him to remain on deck. Turning toward the wheel, Anthony saw the second lieutenant and called him over.

"Mr. Earl, you have the watch. Secure from quarters if you please."

"Aye, Captain."

Anthony's urge got the better of his judgment, so he headed to his cabin with Bart trailing. Anthony raised a finger to his lips to silence the marine sentry from calling out and announcing the captain's presence to all.

Anthony could hear loud voices coming from his cabin as he eased the door open. Lieutenant Witzenfeld's high shrill voice was very distinctive. "He disobeyed my order, my direct order. He was insubordinate and insolent. I want him flogged-flogged do you hear? I've ordered it. A midshipman can't countermand my order or talk to me like that. I've ordered him flogged and flogged he'll be. I'll do my best to see him out of the service for his insolence."

"Dammit, man shut up!" Buck shouted. "Do you have no need to catch a breath?" Lieutenant Buck found himself wiping Witzenfeld's spittle from his face. "I declare sir, you need to get a hold of yourself. You've sprayed all in your path with your damn spittle, and I for one have had enough of your outburst."

"Gawd," Buck exclaimed, his handkerchief busy wiping spittle from his face and coat. "Have you forgotten whom you are addressing?" Buck then called for Paul, the master-at-arms, "Escort Mr. Anthony to the cockpit if you please. I'll be there directly."

"You there," Buck called, addressing the gun crew, "Go see the purser. Give him my compliments, and tell him I'd be grateful if he'd give you all a tot."

The gun crew's eyes lit up, "Thank you sir," they said in unison.

"Mind you now," Buck continued, "There you stay till I send for you."

"Aye sir," each acknowledging his instructions.

Buck then turned his attention back to Lieutenant Witzenfeld, who was still stammering and sputtering to himself. "Go to the wardroom and have a glass of wine," Buck ordered. "You need to get hold of your emotions and pull yourself together, and then we'll talk."

"But sir," argued Witzenfeld, "I don't need to pull myself together. I have the smug bastard where I want him and he'll pay for his ways, captain's brother or not."

Still standing at the entrance to his cabin, Anthony felt himself tremble upon hearing his brother called a bastard. He started through the door only to feel Bart's hand restraining him.

Witzenfeld had continued his tirade, "The captain has no choice. He'll have to flog him. It's time that young gentleman gets his comeuppance. I've promised him a flogging."

"Gawd dammit, man!" Buck was frustrated and about to lose his temper. "You don't flog a midshipman, they're caned. Now I've given you an order and you've not obeyed! You can be arrested, you know. Now go as I've instructed."

Anthony entered his cabin as Witzenfeld fled, not even realizing he passed his captain. Upon his entrance into the cabin, Buck approached Anthony. "Should've set him adrift, sir."

"Pray tell, Rupert," Anthony addressed his first lieutenant. "What's the reason for Witzenfeld's hostility toward Gabe? Is it a way to get to me? Surely, he knows I can only be pushed so far."

"Aye, Captain, he knows. But he also knows, like it or not, that being the captain, you must act accordingly when it comes to regulations. There's no room for family bias, so to speak." Buck then excused himself to go interview the gun crew.

Anthony turned to Bart, "Go talk with Dagan and see if you can discover the basis for Witzenfeld's vendetta."

As Bart left, Silas approached Anthony with a glass. "A little something to settle you, sir."

Anthony took the glass thankfully.

Buck and Bart returned almost simultaneously. Buck returned from talking with the gun crew and Bart from talking with Dagan. Buck related his findings first.

"Witz had given the order to fire the larboard gun. As the gun captain went to fire, Gabe shouted, 'Belay! Hold your fire.' It seems one of the gun crew had stumbled and fallen with his leg behind the carriage wheel. Had the gun been fired, Dawkins would have had his leg crushed. When the gun didn't fire as ordered, Witz shouted, 'I said fire!' Gabe shouted 'Wait!' By that time, the gun crew was helping Dawkins to his feet. Gabe was trying to explain to Witz about Dawkins' falling, but Witz wouldn't hear it. According to the gun crew, he started ranting and raving like a madman. He kept cutting off Gabe's attempt to explain the situation and further ignored the gun captain as he tried to reason with Witz-who in his raving called Gabe a spoiled whoreson. Every man in the gun crew heard it. They also heard Gabe say, 'Witz, if you were a man, I'd call you out and take pleasure in running you through. If only you were a man.' That's when the master-at-arms was summoned."

Anthony looked at Bart who said, "I can explain the 'if you were a man!' According to Dagan, Mr. Witz and Gabe were both on the Revenue Cutter *Raven*. Mr. Witz, being the senior, and Gabe a supernumerary. Admiral Lord Anthony was a friend with Lieutenant Kent, who commanded *Raven* and got Gabe his billet. The smugglers were having a hey-day against the revenue men, and they were frustrated. Witz and Gabe went down to the local tavern for a wet. After a few, Witz started bragging in a loud voice about what he would do if he could just come face-to-face with the smuggler's leader. The rum had loosened Witz's tongue. He said the smugglers were a thieving bunch of whoreson cowards, who were making a mockery of the King's taxes. Gabe noticed Dagan motioning to him at the tavern door. Dagan had with him a man who could possibly have information that would help put an end to some of the smuggling. The man was a relation on Gabe's mother's side. Gabe shushed Witz, and then walked outside to talk with the informant. No sooner had Gabe stepped outside, than a man who had been sitting behind Witz, turned around and calmly jerked him to his feet and laid a sharp blade to his Adam's apple."

"So given the chance you'd gut a smuggler, same as a mackerel, would you?" the man taunted Witz, who was standing on his toes to keep the knifepoint from sticking him. He already had a trickle of blood where the smuggler had made his 'point' as it were. About that time, the tavern wench bent double, slapping her knees and laughing.

"Bess, lass, what's got into you girl?" the smuggler asked. "Are you touched?"

The laughing girl replied, "Look at the brave 'revenoor' man. "'E's pissed 'is pants 'e has!" Sure enough, the entire front of Witz's pants was wet and a puddle was forming at his feet. The entire tavern erupted in laughter. Witz had made a laughing stock of himself. Hearing the commotion inside, Gabe and Dagan hurried back in.

Gabe had taken his pistol out, "Turn him loose." Quiet filled the tavern. "I said turn him loose."

"Ah, Gabe," the smuggler was speaking, "let's not get into a killing over some piss pot that can't even hold his own water."

Gabe gestured with the pistol, "Turn him loose, and then out the back you go."

"Your word?" questioned the smuggler.

"My word," answered Gabe.

The smuggler released his grip on Witz and turned to go. No sooner had Witz been released than his hand flew to his sword. A metallic rasp filled the air as Witz's sword cleared the scabbard and he cried, "I'll kill you!"

The smuggler turned and spat in disgust, "Your word, huh!" He then noticed Gabe was now pointing his pistol toward Witz.

"Let it go, Witz."

"Damned if I will. He humiliated me...a King's officer."

"You're alive, let it go!"

"No," cried Witz. The sound of Gabe cocking his pistol instantly gained Witz's attention.

"I said let it go. I gave my word."

"Witz bolted from the tavern and back to the

cutter. Word spread quickly about Witz losing control of his bladder. Lieutenant Kent had no choice but to have Witz replaced, as he had become the laughing stock of the town. It appears Witz has had it in for Gabe since then."

***

"YES SIR! THAT'S THE way it were Cap'n. Had young Gabe, pardon sir, had Mr. Anthony not stopped it, I'd lost me timber fer sure when the gun went off. I've seen it happen, sir, same as you, I'm sure."

"Thank you, Dawkins," Anthony said. "I'll weigh your comments heavily in my decision. You are dismissed."

The old sailor was almost out the door when he turned and said, "T'wernt no use in Mr. Witz acting so, sir. I been to sea more 'n thirty years, man and boy, and I ain't see'd the like sir. Just wanted ye to know, sir." The wizened old sailor continued on his way.

Anthony had just finished his formal inquiry into the incident. Dawkins had been the last witness. Gabe was guilty all right, but of trying to save an old man's leg and maybe his life. A better, more experienced officer would have looked at the situation, tried to make something positive of Gabe's initiative, and been glad they'd not crippled a good seaman. Witz was neither experienced nor mature enough to put his petty differences aside for the good of the ship and crew. Anthony looked at Buck, who had been standing quietly since Dawkins had left.

"Rupert, old friend, would you be so kind as to summon Lieutenant Witzenfeld?"

"Aye, Captain," Buck said and left the cabin. He couldn't ever recall the captain calling him 'old friend.' A sign of weakness? No. No one could ever call the captain weak. Friendship, he was the captain's friend. Buck suddenly felt very privileged to be considered Anthony's friend, especially when the captain was at his wit's end.

Buck had sent Paul, the master-at-arms, to find Witz and inform him of the captain's summons. He was then to go to the cockpit for Mr. Anthony.

"Allow Witz plenty of time with the captain before you bring Mr. Anthony aft," Buck had whispered to Paul.

The salty old sea dog looked at the first lieutenant, "Give 'im time 'ta feel the heat for awhile, is 'at what we's after, sir?" Buck only nodded as Paul ambled off, amazed at how the old sailor always seemed to have a quid of "baccy" causing his right cheek to bulge to gigantic proportions. A permanent brown stain seemed to fill the crease at the corner of Paul's mouth. Yet Buck could not remember ever having seen the man spit. Recalling his own youthful experiment with "chaw-baccy", Buck could only imagine what was happening to Paul's innards.

Silas had poured Anthony another of his coffee brandy concoctions. "Ta steel yourself, sir," he said by way of explanation. "His kind ain't worth loosen ya temper over."

"The first lieutenant, sir," the marine had barely gotten the announcement past his lips when the cry from above was heard.

"Man overboard! Man overboard!" Lieutenant Earl was already turning the ship by the time Anthony and Buck hurried on deck.

***

"WELL, AT LEAST THAT'S a chapter that's closed," Buck said. "And I for one am glad." The man overboard had been Lieutenant Witzenfeld. Every effort had been made to recover the man but to no avail. The bosun had said, "He musta headed straight fer Davy Jones locker from the onset. No bobbin' or cries like you'd expect from a man trying to stay afloat."

The quartermaster, who had been at the wheel when the incident happened, tried to explain what he saw. "'E 'ad a fit 'e did, sir, went berserk. He was acting like a madman, just a slobbering like and flinging his arms about, like 'e was swatting at bees, sir. Screaming 'is bloody head off saying the devil was on him. 'E was touched sir, so 'e was, just plain touched. It put a scare in me, Cap'n. I ain't shamed to say it. No sir, it was frightful."

When things on deck had settled down, Anthony and Buck had the opportunity to talk with Peckham who had also seen the incident. "Witz was headed aft to report to you," the master explained. "Dagan was standing close to the hatch, outta the wind, so he could light his pipe. As Witz approached the companionway, he appeared startled and upset to find Dagan standing there. He gave Dagan an angry scowl. Dagan looked up from lighting his pipe and said, 'Careful where thy step, sir. Accidents happen, a misstep could haunt you a lifetime.'

"Well, sir, Witz turned ghost white pale. He let go a scream to make yer blood curdle. 'Twere like the banshee was after him. Like the quartermaster said, it was over the side he went. You know the rest."

Anthony had let the master tell his story without interruption. Then he asked, "Tell me, Mr. Peckham, would you consider Dagan's words a threat to Lieutenant Witzenfeld?"

"Nay, Cap'n. More like a friendly reminder I'd say."

Long after everyone had gone, Anthony lay in his cot looking at the deck beams overhead. He found himself taking in all the sounds a ship at sea will make. The water sluicing down the hull as the bow plunged through another wave. The gentle groan of timbers as they were being flexed as the ship cut through a trough only to have its bow lifted by a swell. The sound of the watch on deck, all familiar but distant. In the stillness, Anthony's body gave a sudden shiver and once again he could hear his father's old servant whisper, "He's a soothsayer, sir. A sorcerer."

Chapter Five

ANTHONY WOKE WITH THE foul taste of cheap wine and bad cigars. His head felt worse than his mouth tasted. He had been a guest of the wardroom last evening, and this morning he was paying for the merriment. Since the incident with Witzenfeld, the ship had seemed different. The crew seemed happier and more content. Anthony had heard some go so far as to say "can't say's I'm sorry he's gone." Well to be honest, neither was he. Gabe was now acting fourth lieutenant and so far all seemed well. Gabe and Earl had performed for the wardroom last evening. Some of their renditions were lewd and provocative. The wardroom officers laughed at each attempt as Gabe and Earl set to music some profane rhyme, one trying to outdo the other. The surgeon was the judge and proclaimed neither winner nor loser, but a draw.

Silas entered with coffee and hot water for Anthony's shave. "The Master says if his calculations are on, we'll likely see land by the end of the first dog watch. It's a good thing too, sir. With Mr. Buck dropping in as 'e does, we've just about run outta coffee."

Anthony grunted, "You and Bart don't tip a cup now and then do you?"

"Occasionally we does," answered the servant. "If you've 'ad yer fill and they's a swallow left in the pot, we's don't like to see it go to waste."

"I'm sure," Anthony said.

Bart had entered the cabin, "Dawn's almost on us, sir. It's sweltering already and the master says we're shaping up for a squall. Mr. Pitts got the watch, sir. He's dancing around like a whore in church. He's got one eye on the horizon and the other watching aft for you."

This brought a smile to Anthony. Someone else undoubtedly was feeling the worse from last evening's merriment. After far too many glasses of wine, Mr. Pitts had stood to make a toast before ending the evening's festivities. He was too much in his cups, and when the ship was hit by a large swell, the roll of the ship threw Pitts off balance and he sprawled headlong onto the wardroom table. The surgeon had pronounced him "drunk for the evening." Anthony could only imagine how embarrassed the young officer felt. If Anthony had been in his place, he'd certainly keep a weather eye out for the captain until he saw how he fared after last night's actions.

The master was in conversation with Pitts when Anthony came on deck. The wind was picking up. Dawn was breaking all right. Anthony could already make out faces of the men working forward. One of the seamen commented to no one in particular, "Was that a lightning flash off the larboard bow?"

Markham, the now senior midshipman, volunteered, "I thought I heard thunder too."

Anthony turned quickly. Anger rose in his eyes as he addressed Pitts. "Thunder be damned, that's cannon fire! Are the lookouts asleep, sir?"

Pitts called up to the masthead lookout who said, "I 'ears it now sir, and seed a flash but thought it was lightning. Nothing more's visible yet." Pitts turned to his captain, "Clear for action, sir?"

"No, not yet," Anthony replied. "Send for the first lieutenant."

"Here I am, Captain."

Turning, Anthony saw Buck. "Well good morning, Mr. Buck. I hate to see that your rest was disturbed after such a hearty evening, but I fear the day promises to be an active one. We'll go ahead and have the crew fed an early breakfast."

"Aye, Captain," the officers on the quarterdeck answered in unison.

Bart was there with Anthony's sword and pistols. "Let's go finish our coffee, Bart. There will be time for them directly," Anthony said, speaking of his weapons. Halfway down the companionway Anthony called back to Buck, "After breakfast send Dagan to the masthead with a glass. Let's see if his peepers are as good as my father claimed them to be."

***

AN AIR OF EXCITEMENT and expectation seemed to hover on deck as Anthony returned from breaking his fast. It was much lighter and all the lieutenants and young gentlemen seemed to be about. The crew moved with just a little bounce in their step. *Someone must have mentioned the possibility of prize money*, Anthony thought.

Dagan had proved his worth. With Anthony's return on deck, Buck reported to him, "Looks like a pair of topsail schooners, bearing down on a barque. They don't appear to be friendly."

"They don't appear to be friendly?" Anthony asked.

"No sir. They're flying the red flag-no mercy, no quarter. One schooner's to leeward, and the other to windward. It's like one was lying in wait and chased the barque toward the open arms of the other."

"Have they seen us yet?" Anthony asked.

"They've shown no sign they have, Captain. The sun is behind us so we would be hard to see, especially when they're so engrossed with the prospect of plunder."

"Well, let's see if we can give them something else to chew on," Anthony said. "Beat to quarters if you will, Mr. Buck."

"The barque's in range so why ain't they firing on her?" Mr. Davy asked. Both Anthony and Buck turned to the young middy. Since Witz had cast his lot to the depths, the once introverted boy seemed to have blossomed. However, butt-ing in when his betters were in discussion would see him "kissing the gunner's daughter." Bart intervened before things went too far.

"Begging the captain's pardon, but I believe the young gentlemen is needed forward, sir."

Anthony knew an old sea dog like Bart would educate the boy on when it was proper to speak and when not. He'd also explain that pirates would rather take a ship with as little damage to the spoils as possible.

Dagan cried down from the masthead, "One of the schooners has come together with the barque and appears to be grappling, sir. The other's closing in fast."

"Very well. Mr. Earl."

"Aye, Captain."

"Soon as you think proper, fire a ranging shot and see if we can give the buggers something else to think on."

"Aye, sir," Earl answered, and then he went forward.

"Do you want Dagan down, sir?"

"No, Mr. Buck, not yet."

The air was tense and everyone seemed to be holding their collective breath. This would be their first action under a new captain. The gun captain assigned to the cannon nearest to where Anthony was standing bent over to peer out the gun port. As he did so, he loosened a thunderous round of flatulence.

Anthony, taken aback by the man's 'outburst,'

cried out, "Damme sir, but I don't recall having given the order to fire!"

The crew roared with laughter.

"Silence," Buck ordered, but even he couldn't keep a straight face.

The offender sheepishly said, "I beg the captain's pardon, sir."

BOOM! The long nine rebounded against its lashing.

"A hit," Dagan called down.

"Damn if Mr. Earl doesn't know his business," Anthony said to Buck.

"Aye sir. That'll get the whoresons' attention all right."

BOOM!

"Another hit," Dagan called down again. "They know we're about now, sir." No sooner had Dagan spoken than the windward schooner returned fire.

"That was damn quick," said Peckham, wiping spray from his face. The schooner's first ball had been just short of its target.

"A bit too accurate for my liking too," said the quartermaster at the wheel. Anthony called to Mr. Earl, "Let them taste a complete broadside if you please."

"Aye, Captain," Earl said. Turning to the gun crew, he said, "Let's give 'em what for, lads. On the up roll now fire, fire as you bear."

An entire broadside was unleashed as *Drakkar's* cannons breathed fire. Earl had fired on the up roll to try and prevent as much collateral damage as possible to the barque. Still, the shots fell like a raining hell, and several balls found their mark. Great pieces of bulwark were seen flying through the air. Anthony knew the schooners were fragile and could not take such an onslaught much longer.

The wind had veered to directly astern. It carried the smoke from *Drakkar's* broadside with it, making visibility difficult.

"Hands to braces, Mr. Buck. We'll close with them now."

"Aye, sir. Bosun hands to braces!"

Drakkar swung around and was now on a converging tack with the three ships. Dagan, still at the masthead, called down, "One of the schooners has loosened her grapnels and is casting off, but she's dragging her bowsprit."

Anthony had a sudden notion. "Mr. Buck, have a couple of boats made ready with a sizable boarding party. We'll drop them off as we pass by the schooner that's still grappled to the barque. Have the boats lowered on the larboard side. Now, put the best gunners on the starboard side and have them load with grape. I want to cut down on the black legs as we pass making it easier for our boarding party. Tell the gunners to fire as they bear! Then we'll beat down to the other cutthroat."

"Aye, Captain," Buck said and turned to organize the boarding party.

"Oh, Mr. Buck."

"Yes sir!"

"Have Dagan come down. I'm sure we have a better use for him at this point."

Buck couldn't help but smile. He couldn't see Gabe getting into a boat for a boarding party without Dagan.

The fleeing schooner fired again. They were closing the gap quicker than Anthony realized. *Drakkar's* fore topgallant mast came tumbling down. Part of the jib ripped and flapped in the breeze with a loud pop.

"Damned feist," cried Peckham.

"That feist's still got teeth," Anthony responded.

Drakkar made her own response with another broadside. The schooner seemed to shudder as *Drakkar's* twenty-four pounders struck home. The mainmast was carried away and acted like a great sea anchor almost stopping the schooner in her wake. The remaining sails were full of shot holes. The fo'c'sle and bulwark had great gaps thanks to *Drakkar's* gunners.

"Give the bastards a taste of grape, Mr. Buck. We'll then board and see if there's any life left in them." Anthony had to give the pirates credit for their bravery. He knew the loss of life on board the schooner had to be great...but better them than his crew. They had already condemned themselves.

The range was now less than two cables. One

by one the guns discharged their load of iron death as they came to bear. When the guns were silent, Anthony realized he'd been holding his hands over his ears to protect them from the deafening sound of cannon fire.

The schooner was now alongside. Anthony could see tiny splinters leap up from the deck as musket balls were being fired from the pirates' rigging. One of the gun captains cried out, and then clenched his teeth as a ball tore into his shoulder. His mate was not so lucky. A ball tore into his face and plucked out one eyeball and part of his skull.

"Sharpshooter. Has the damnable fellow got sharpshooters, Mr. Buck?"

"I don't know if there are sharpshooters, Captain, but the foretops are full of them. Whatever they be."

"By the volley fire!" Lieutenant Dunn's marines were responding. He was pointing to the foretops with his sword. The pirates fell from the marines' accuracy. Dunn, in his Scottish accent, could be heard directing his marines to their next target. Because the schooner alongside was a smaller ship, *Drakkar's* marines were having a heyday firing down onto the pirates below them. The last volley cleared a mob of pirates that had gathered in the waist.

"Boarders, away!" Anthony had his sword out, as did Buck. Bart had armed himself with a tomahawk and his cutlass. The freshly sharpened blade glinted in the sunlight. Grapnels had locked the ships together, and *Drakkar's* boarders half-slid, half- jumped down on the schooner's deck.

Anthony landed with a grunt. He slipped and, peering down, saw he'd landed on a dead pirate's innards. A huge pirate took his mind off the gore by screaming obscenities and attacking him with a boarding pike. Bart dispatched the pirate with his tomahawk, but no sooner was the man down than Anthony found himself facing two more pirates. One was a foul-smelling, hawkish man. Anthony shot him at point blank range with his pistol. As the man's face turned to a bloody pulp, his mate was upon Anthony with a boarding pike and cutlass. The man was strong, but slow. He reeked of rum, perspiration, and death. Fighting the brute, Anthony found himself in the center of a melee. He was being bumped, prodded and lashed from a number of directions. A wounded pirate fell from the rigging and slammed into Anthony, causing him to fall to one knee. As he did, he raised his blade to deflect a blow from another pirate's cutlass. The shock numbed his shoulder. However, swinging with such force threw the big oaf off-balance, opening his guard. Anthony thrust upward, with all of his strength, driving his sword through the man's neck. A fountain of blood gushed out, spraying Anthony. The air reeked as the smell of gun smoke intertwined with the salt air and rancid smell of blood and death. Shouts and groans that turned into hysterical screams, the thud-like sound as a boarding pike crushed a skull, gunshots, and metal against metal sounded as men fought with blades. Desperate men all fighting to live.

Drakkar's boarders now had the upper hand. They had pushed the remaining pirates to the aft rail. Lieutenant Dunn's marines held them at bay with muskets and bayonets. The defeated pirates finally threw down their weapons in surrender.

***

The two schooners were *LeFoxxe* and *LeCroix*. Both were French named, but crewed by a motley group of various descriptions. Some wore jackboots while others were barefooted. A few sported colorful sashes tied about their waist while others were naked from the waist up. All appeared to be vicious brutes, now doomed for the hangman's knot.

The barque was a private ship, The *Royal Chatham*, bound for Barbados. Her captain, officers, and many of the crew and passengers were dead. Anthony could still recall the look of dismay on their faces as Gabe and Earl described the scene they'd encountered as they boarded the ship.

The deck was soaked in blood. The pirates were in a frenzy and had not only killed but had mutilated the bodies. The ship owner's wife, Lady Deborah McKean, had been forced to watch as her husband and servant girl had been murdered. The servant girl had been stripped, repeatedly raped, then had her breasts cut off. Two pirates had joked as they fondled the breasts, remarking on what fine "purses" they'd make.

Anthony had inquired, "Is the lady well?"

"Aye," replied Earl. "As good as she can be after witnessing the horror and hell the pirates made her watch."

"They gutted Lord McKean like a mackerel," Gabe had said. "It's a good thing we arrived when we did. Otherwise...," he swallowed and then changed the subject. "The surgeon is doing what he can for the survivors now, sir."

"Good," said Anthony. "When they're able to be moved, have them brought on board *Drakkar*."

***

ANTHONY WALKED TO THE starboard side rail. He'd heard the quartermaster's whisper to warn the watch "cap'n on deck." Anthony peered over the rail and into the Caribbean waters. The sparkle of the phosphorus on the black water; with the moon shining down; made him melancholy. It had only been thirty-six hours or so since they'd engaged the pirates and captured the two schooners. Time had been taken to make the needed repairs before proceeding on to Antigua. The sound of the carpenter's saws and hammers still seem to vibrate in Anthony's head. Looking aft, he could barely see the nearest prize as it followed in *Drakkar's* wake. From the time Lady McKean had come on board he'd felt a strange tightness in his chest. It was like something he'd never experienced...an attraction to the woman...the widow. He was uneasy with this new sensation. He was a King's officer, and shouldn't be moping like a schoolboy. The poor woman had gone through so much. She'd had to watch as her husband was so brutally murdered. He should be feeling sorry for her, feeling sympathy. But dammit, she stirred him, and they'd barely even spoken. As would be expected, he offered her his cabin-a gesture appropriate for a lady of her status. It was the least he could do, given the tragedy and horror she had just experienced. Silas had fussed over her proper like. She had been Anthony's dinner guest that evening. Silas had prepared a simple, but tasty supper. The first they had taken together since she come aboard *Drakkar.*

Silas first served a light wine with cheese and nuts to create the appetite. He then brought out a ragout of pork, carrots, and pureed potatoes. The butter was starting to taste a little old but it was still good with the bread Silas had kept warm by putting a hot brick wrapped in a cloth next to it. Anthony knew he was doing his best to impress the lady when for dessert he surprised them with a dish of his special apple tarts. These were almost as famous as his coffee and the two went well together.

The meal had been very subdued...polite, but quiet. Yet there was something there, drawing him to her. He could still smell the faint odor of her perfume as it lingered on the night air interlaced with the familiar scents of the sea. Anthony found himself peering aft again. Buck had taken command of the barque. Mr. Earl had one schooner, and Gabe, with a master's mate, had the other.

What a sight they would make entering harbour. The *Royal Chatham* would be recognized immediately. This would start tongues wagging. He could envision the signals from the flag officer already. Questions would certainly be raised. Was it simply bad luck that the *Royal Chatham* had fallen into the clutches of two pirates working together? Some would wonder if there might be an accomplice ashore, a traitor, who had sent word so that the pirates would be lying in wait for the barque and its rich cargo. Was someone getting rich from his share of the booty, but without endangering himself in open battle. If there were such a person, he was obviously shrewd, and dangerous. Anthony's mind drifted back to the "prizes" and Gabe.

Gabe had reported a large sum of gold, silver, and jewels, as well as other valuables, in the captain's cabin on board the schooner he had boarded. Anthony couldn't help but feel some of the "treasure" may not have made it aboard *Drakkar*.

When Gabe had been asked how much loot had been found, his answer seemed somewhat evasive, "Too much to count, sir."

Dagan had spoken up, an act which was rare in itself. "Aye, too much to count, and no record to go by, sir."

Anthony thought that without proper re-
cords, he had nothing to account for. The Admiralty would be very grateful for what he had
recovered. Still, he wondered if Gabe and Dagan
didn't profit from a wee bit of larceny.

Chapter Six

ANTIGUA WAS A SMALL island, but was great in regards to the needs of the Royal Navy in the West Indies. As dawn's light lit the early sky, the master's predictions came true. The island seemed to creep up over the horizon until it was in plain view. This made old Peckham strut like a peacock. Anthony never doubted the master's prediction, and was just as excited as he at having made a perfect landfall. It had been nearly six weeks since they had left England. Not a speed record by any means, but the time had been well used. The crew's sail handling had been tested in all kinds of weather conditions. They had become proficient with the guns, and now *Drakkar* was battle tested. Not much of a battle to be sure, but for a first action Anthony was more than pleased. The crew had been seasoned, and had grown together and now was a fighting unit. There had been one flogging, but this was expected. On most ships there would have been many more. Except for Witzenfeld, the passage had been a perfect training exercise.

As the sun rose, the sky became cloudless. The deep blue Caribbean seemed to invite and welcome the frigate into her waters. Sea gulls and all manner of other birds were everywhere, swooping down, gawking and then darting off. At times, they seemed to hover in one spot, and then flapping their wings, they'd fly away. Anthony sensed someone's presence. Turning, he stood face to face with Lady McKean. In spite of the warm sun, she gave a shiver. Unpleasant memories of Antigua? Recalling the recent ordeal? Anthony was left to wonder.

His own thoughts had drifted that way. They had lost five crewmembers, discharged dead, and another five or six had significant, but not life threatening wounds. Not so terrible a price to pay in the overall scheme of things but while thankful of the few losses, his heart went out to those who had lost their lives. The Admiralty would consider the losses negligible compared to the schooners they'd captured. Especially given all the head money and specie they had retrieved.

Lady McKean would find no solace in this however. "Will we have time to speak after we anchor, Captain?"

"I'm sure, my lady," Anthony replied. "I have to report to the flag officer, if he's in port. I'm sure I'll have to meet with the commissioner at the dockyard. However, after the official visits, I'm sure we'll have time to visit before *Drakkar* sails."

"I would be grateful, Captain," Lady McKean replied.

"Gil, my lady. Please just call me Gil."

Pausing, Lady McKean looked at Anthony, "If you insist. I know you have much to attend to without me in the way." Then she was gone.

***

"DECK THERE," THE MASTHEAD lookout called down. "Several ships anchored just off the headland, sir. One's a second-rate, at least."

"That'll be the flag ship," Anthony remarked to the master as he approached. "Make a signal to Buck and the two schooners to standby to fire salute."

"Aye, Cap'n."

"Mr. Pitts."

"Here sir."

"Prepare to wear ship."

"Aye, sir."

"Once that's completed, begin the salute."

"Yes, sir," Mr. Pitts answered, and then dashed away to attend his duties.

"Bout to bust, he is, with his newfound authority," Peckham remarked to Anthony as soon as Pitts was out of hearing. "Better watch out, Cap'n, or he'll be admiral before you."

"I'm sure," Anthony replied. "I'm going down to change. No doubt the Admiral will signal before the anchor's let go. Bart?"

"Here Cap'n, I'm already preparing the gig, sir."

***

ANTIGUA WAS THE ROYAL Navy's headquarters

and main base in the West Indies. As Gabe strode across the quarterdeck of the schooner, *LeCroix,* he thought of his father. He had spent many an evening listening as the admiral had told stories and shared his memories of Antigua and the West Indies with Dagan and him. Hopefully, he'd have some to share when this commission was over.

The West Indies was a chain of islands on the eastern side of the Caribbean. These islands were full of natural harbours and inlets, making for the perfect lair of pirates. Therefore, opportunities for someone such as he should be abundant. Since Witz's death, Gabe had been made acting fourth lieutenant. If luck held, he'd make lieutenant before too long. It was not unthinkable that once he made lieutenant he might even be given command of some little prize...like this schooner.

Thinking of "this little prize" made him think of Dagan. *How much loot did he confiscate before letting anyone know it had been found? Better yet, where did he hide it?* "For us'en in case of a cloudy day" was all Dagan said, as he took a small chest and placed it aside before letting anyone know of their "find." He had handed Gabe a large red ruby that had to be ten carats or more. "For luck," Dagan said. Gabe didn't like keeping this from Anthony, but he didn't want to say anything to hurt Dagan either.

Gabe fondled the gem in his coat pocket, and

thought of the articles of war. He felt a chill run through him. "For luck," Dagan said. *Well, he damn well hoped good luck was all that ever came of it*, Gabe thought.

Dagan approached and said, "*Drakkar's* signaling."

Gabe responded without even thinking, "Look alive men. The admjral's eyes are upon us. We don't want him to liken us to a bunch of bum boatsmen."

The winds had backed to the southeast. *Drakkar* was leaving a white wake in the blue sea. Even under reduced sail, she appeared a force with which to be reckoned. She glided into the harbour, having completed the salute. The anchor had scarcely been loosened when the admiral's signal 'repair on board' had been hoisted. Anthony was proud of how well Bart had the gig's crew turned out. Of course, he'd expected no different. Even Mr. Davy was turned out smart as a bullock on parade day. He had been brought along to carry dispatches.

"Bloody worthless little shit if you ask me," Bart had said. Anthony knew his comments were a ruse. Bart had taken to the young gentleman and had spent hours 'educating' the lad. Even now, he was explaining to Davy the age-old tradition of 'the captain is last into the boat but first out.' Davy was listening to Bart, but couldn't help but gawk at the flagship. He had thought *Drakkar* big, but the flagship was gigantic to the young mid.

Robert Harvey was flag captain of *HMS Namur*. She was small for a second rate...only ninety guns. However, she could still provide deadly force. Harvey met Anthony as he came on board, shaking his hand even before honors had been completed. After pleasantries had been exchanged, the two talked captain to captain. "Sir Lawrence Finylson, Rear-admiral of the Blue, is our lord and master. He has tried very hard to deal with this pestilence of pirates and privateers. However, until you arrived, he had only one frigate...a small twenty-eight. It's a wonder she still floats, her hull is so wormy. We've lost a couple of brigs, and a hurricane damaged our one sloop so badly she will have to be completely overhauled. There's little enough left to justify our admiral's presence. He's tried with what little resources we have, but Sir Lawrence is ill and grows tired. Now that you're here, I expect he'll haul down his flag so he can go back to England and enjoy what little time he has left."

When Anthony was ushered into the admiral's stateroom by the flag lieutenant, he was shocked. The man before him looked very tired and old. Yellow Jack had taken its toll on the old admiral.

"Ah, Gil, how are you? Have a seat." The admiral then ordered the flag lieutenant to fetch some ice. As soon as the man left, the admiral jokingly remarked, "Soon as he gets back, we'll have a cool glass of refreshment, that is if he doesn't get lost and let the ice melt before he returns." Anthony had to smile. The admiral may be getting up in years, but he still maintained a good humor.

"I looked through the reports while you and Harvey were talking. Bad business with Lieutenant Witzenfeld. Demons, demons, I tell you. They take a man's soul and torment him to the point of madness. Worse than with drink. I've seen it happen, right here on this island. Demons, pure and simple. Some of the locals call it voodoo or something like that."

"Now about those damnable pirates." The admiral had changed tack so quickly Anthony was momentarily confused. "It appears you dished them up prim and proper. Wee bit of prize money and head money too. You'll need those prizes, and so we'll buy them into the service. Oh, before I forget. Did we get an accurate count on the value of the treasure?"

"Not yet, sir. We've been rather busy," answered Anthony.

"Well, get to it when you can."

"Aye sir," Anthony replied.

"A very lucky beginning for you, Gil. More than I've had in three years. I've decided to haul down my flag. I'm sending my request on the next packet. I'm also going to appoint you to commodore. Of course, the Admiralty will have to confirm the appointment, but I don't see any problem there. What say you? I was very sorry to hear about Lord McKean." The admiral had changed tack again without even pausing or taking a deep breath. "He was a good man. They had no children, so that leaves Lady McKean alone and a prime catch, if I do say so. She was years younger than Lord McKean. You're not married are you, Gil?"

"Er–no, sir," replied Anthony, somewhat taken aback by the admiral's frankness.

***

ONCE BACK ON *DRAKKAR*, Anthony's officers were jubilant over the news of his being appointed commodore.

"Yer broad pennant, sir. It's about time," Buck said.

Anthony looked at his first lieutenant and said, "Yes, but it would have been better if I could have had a captain under me. You know you would have been my choice."

"Aye, Captain, but don't worry. White ball below the pennant or not, we'll show 'em. And when we're through you'll be flying your own flag, and that's no error."

Once the excitement over Anthony's broad pennant subsided, he, Buck and the master discussed his findings on the flagship. "Those blackguards are no match for us on the open sea. However, once we're sighted, they make for the closest island, cay, inlet, or reef where we can't follow. According to Captain Harvey, we've lost two brigs. Laid their keels open on a reef trying to catch the cutthroats."

"Amateurs," snorted Peckham.

Anthony cut a glance at the old master. "Well, amateurs or not, we'll need those two schooners to use, not unlike a terrier after a rabbit."

"How will we man them, sir?" Buck asked.

"We can have the survivors off those brigs I mentioned. There's still a few of them around. The rest, Mr. Buck, I leave up to you. I'll expect recommendations on the morrow."

Anthony then turned to the master. "See what you can find in the way of updated charts. I'm sure the locals will have more accurate ones than these," he said. Disgusted, Anthony tossed his calipers on the charts laid across the table before him.

"Now I'll leave these problems in your capable hands. I'll see what the island has to offer in the way of officer's uniforms on my way to meet the dockyard commissioner."

***

ANTHONY LOOKED AT THE envelope with the official seal on the back. "Mr. Markham passed it along, sir," Silas reported. "I didn't disturb you right away as you were plotting with Mr. Buck and the master."

"Plotting?"

"Aye, sir. Ain't that what yews was about? Plotting on how to deal with them sea devils."

Anthony smiled at Silas's description of his meeting with Buck and the master. "Yes, we were plotting, Silas."

The envelope held an invitation to a reception that was being given in *Drakkar's* honor. The reception was to be held at Commodore Gardner, the dockyard commissioner's, residence. Anthony had paid the commodore his official call, but not before he'd acquired his new uniforms. Gardner was a nice enough official who Anthony took a liking to immediately. He'd given his condolences on the loss of Anthony's father.

"We were friends," he said, stating that they were together in Hawke's squadron in '59. "Your father was in command of the *Cambridge* eighty. I had been first lieutenant on the *Edgar* sixty-four. The *Edgar's* captain was killed and I was given command. It rained hell that day...pure hell. It was soon after that your father was given his flag."

***

THERE WAS A SLIGHT ocean breeze blowing when Anthony, Buck, and Gabe got out of the coach. *The rest of the officers, except those on watch, should arrive at any time*, Anthony thought. A black servant, dressed in finery for the evening's festivities, opened the coach's door for them. The ground crunched beneath their shoes. Crushed seashells, long bleached white by the sun, had been used to line the path to the elegant white house. It was set just off the coast road atop a small hill. Anthony was sure it was built here to take advantage of these little breezes that they were now enjoying. Through the wide gates and up the white steps, they were taking it all in. The residence must surely belong to some rich merchant or ship owner and was on loan to the commodore. The commodore would not likely be able to afford such a residence. Anthony was certain the commodore would pass along to the owner any lucrative Royal Navy contracts that were available, thereby making it an advantageous situation for all parties.

Roses and gardenias were everywhere, their blossoms giving off a faint odor that seemed to drape across the light breeze. Another servant, a doorman, opened a pair of large ornate doors. As the three entered the room Anthony whispered, "Watch what you drink. These island brews will put a man's arse hole over a tea kettle before he knows it." Buck and Gabe nodded their acknowledgment, as each was wide-eyed at the splendid dwelling before them.

The room was awash with music and conversation until the door was opened. The sound suddenly hushed as another servant announced, "Lord Gilbert Anthony, Knight of the Bath, commanding His Majesty's frigate, *Drakkar*."

Anthony suddenly felt self-conscious, as if he were on public display. However, no sooner had the introduction been given than the room was a roar again. The commodore was coming to greet him. Gabe, he noticed, had already been encircled by a group of bare shouldered young ladies. No doubt he was calculating his chance of ridding himself of some pent-up humors.

Anthony turned and whispered to Buck before the commodore reached them, "I expect all officers to be back on board by four bells on the morning watch."

"Aye, sir," Buck replied.

Anthony introduced Buck to Commodore Gardner, and then allowed him to wander off in search of a possible "prize" for the evening. The air in the large room was hot and humid. The noise, candles, and body heat from all the mingling guests made it almost oppressive. No wonder the ladies all had small fans and were busily waving with them.

Greta, Commodore Gardner's wife, approached her friend, Lady Deborah McKean. She had been standing in a small vestibule taking in the festivities before her, but her eyes never wandering far before they returned to the British naval captain who commanded the ship which had rescued her.

Greta, watching her friend's gaze, volunteered, "A striking man isn't he? Not overly handsome but he is so commanding he makes you look twice. I felt my heart skip when we were introduced."

Touching Greta's hand, Lady Deborah seemed to tremble.

"A touch of humors?" her friend asked.

"No, it's just that...that, well Greta, we've had no secrets between you and me. I don't want to be disloyal to the memory of Lord McKean, but I feel like...like a young girl when I'm close to Captain Anthony. I think I've found the man I could love."

Greta was touched by her friend's admission, but not surprised. She had known the marriage between Deborah and Lord McKean had been an arrangement. Greta took the glass of wine from her friend's hand and turned her so that they were facing each other.

"Deborah, you listen to me. Lord McKean was a good man but he's dead. Life is short and out here in the islands it's shorter still. You deserve some happiness in your life. Go to him. Let him know how you feel. We can't be assured of tomorrow, so live it for today and to hell with the rest. Besides, some other devilish imp will get her clutches on him if you wait. Now go to him and let him know how you feel. I'll help arrange a discreet meeting later."

Anthony could not for the life of him remember half of the guests' names that the commodore introduced him to. Never had he shaken so many hands or bowed to so many ladies in one evening. Nor could he remember drinking so much. Scarcely had his glass been emptied before it was refilled, or replaced. Anthony's officers were all being entertained like conquering heroes. Much was made of the pirates murdering Lord McKean, and *Drakkar's* sudden arrival. Turning, Anthony spied Buck in deep conversation with a boldly dressed woman. Her bosom was so open it scarcely left anything to the imagination.

Anthony felt a hand on his upper arm. Turning, he felt like the room was spinning. She was here, standing before him. He felt his chest tighten.

"Lady McKean."

"Lord Anthony." She was dressed in black, but still she was here.

"I'm very pleased to see you," Anthony said. "I was not sure you would be here, considering all you've been through."

Lady McKean looked at Anthony, and he was not quite sure how to take her next words. "But sir, you are my rescuer. This reception is in your honor. How could I not be present?" They had moved toward an open window in search of a little breeze. "Did you know my husband?"

Anthony was caught off guard, "Madam?"

"Did you know my husband?" she asked again.

"No, my lady, I never had the honor."

"Lord McKean was of Scottish descent. He came from a titled family of long standing. Titled, but impoverished. Ours was an arranged marriage. My father was a tradesman – a rich, powerful tradesman, but still a tradesman. Being a tradesman meant he wasn't completely accepted as a gentleman. This pained my father. He wanted a son, but he had a daughter. He hoped that by my marriage to Lord McKean, he would have titled grandsons. We had a son but lost him to the fever. I've had no others. Now my son, my father, and my husband are all gone. When we were attacked, we were headed to Barbados to meet some of my husband's friends. They were giving him a birthday party, his seventy-fifth."

Anthony was astounded. Thinking aloud he said, "He was old enough to be your father."

"One year younger than my father," she replied. "I was never quite sure if the reason we didn't have more children was my fault or his. But at his age I felt it might have been his."

Anthony didn't know what to say about this discovery but muttered, "Did you love him?"

Lady McKean looked somewhat hurt, "As I said, ours was an arranged marriage. But after a fashion, I guess I did. He was a good and caring man. He dearly loved me, and so I tried to make him happy. I was faithful."

"Dear God! I should be ashamed of myself," Anthony said. "I have no right."

"You have every right, Gil," Lady McKean said, using his given name. "My dashing captain, sweeping down with cannons blazing away. You have all the right."

Anthony half heard the bell. Dinner was being called, and he could feel the guests closing in.

"I have to see you!"

"I'll send you a message," she replied.

They were then caught up in the crowd headed to the dining room. Looking for his place card, Anthony realized that the admiral was not present. Anthony was seated to the right of Commodore Gardner, and to the left was Harvey, the admiral's flag captain. He looked at Anthony and said, "Sir Lawrence is ill this evening and sends his regrets."

Commodore Gardner made a little speech once again honoring Anthony and the men of *Drakkar* for their bravery and wishing them future success. A toast was then made to recognize Anthony's broad pennant. Then the meal was over. No further contact with Lady McKean had been possible. Anthony had hoped to see her again before the evening was over.

As the more senior officers took their leave from the ladies to enjoy cigars and discuss the situation with the pirates, Anthony observed Gabe, and then Buck, as each departed. Each man left with a beautiful lady on his arm, creating a touch of envy in him. Mr. Markham was much in his cups and was in tow of Mr. Earl. Hopefully, they'd make it back to *Drakkar* safely.

"Well, Lord Anthony, we hope you enjoyed your evening," Mrs. Gardner, the commodore's wife, was saying.

"Er...yes, madam. It was a wonderful evening. Thank you for being such a wonderful hostess."

"Not at all, sir. We must thank you for bringing a little excitement into our lives."

As Anthony took Mrs. Gardner's offered hand, he felt her press a small slip of paper into his hand. He continued his bow and kissed the back of her hand. As Anthony straightened, he thought he caught a wink from Mrs. Gardner.

"I do hope you have a rewarding time while you are at English Harbour, sir."

"Thank you again," Anthony said. He then turned to bid the commodore goodnight.

"Could we lunch tomorrow, Gil?"

"It would be a pleasure, sir," Anthony responded, then walked out into the night. It was warm outside, but still much cooler than it had been inside the house.

Bart was standing beside the coach as Anthony approached. "It's not far over to the jetty, sir, if you care to stretch your legs. I has yer pipe and Dagan gave me some good smelling tobaccy."

"Good idea, Bart," Anthony said, taking the pipe. Bart had already filled the bowl so he lit up and they started their journey down the hill.

"Ye seems to be in a good mood tonight, sir. It appears things are to ya likin'."

"Aye, Bart that it is. This island may have some promise to it."

Bart looked at Anthony. "I left Dagan at the jetty. We 'ad us a wet or two together and now he's waiting on Gabe."

"Might be a long wait," Anthony answered.

"Nay, Dagan says 'ell be along in an hour."

"He does, does he?"

"Aye," Bart said. "Dagan also said we'd be seeing some big changes in you soon."

"Is that so?"

"Aye!"

"Any specifics?"

"Nay, I didn't ask and 'e didn't 'laborate."

Anthony looked at Bart smiling, "You mean he didn't elaborate."

"Nay, 'e didn't 'laborate a' tall."

Anthony took another puff on his pipe, tasting the gentle sweetness of Dagan's tobacco. He watched as the smoke drifted on the wind, the aroma of the tobacco intermingling with the smell of salt in the air. Watching the smoke rise and fade away as he exhaled, Anthony pondered Dagan's predictions. Could it have anything to do with the paper in his pocket? Could Dagan really see the future? Was he a soothsayer?

Chapter Seven

FOUR BELLS IN THE forenoon watch the next day found Anthony, his officers, warrants, and midshipmen gathered around his dining table for a meeting. Silas, with the help of a wardroom servant, was pouring lime juice as refreshment. Anthony nodded to Buck to go ahead and start with the meeting. Buck shuffled some papers around, and then stepped forward.

"With Commodore Gardner and Captain Harvey's help, I've been able to round up forty odd hands. With the likelihood that Sir Lawrence will haul down his flag soon, we might pick up a few more sailors who have married and put down roots here. The two schooners are so alike I take them to be sister ships built by the same shipyard. Mr. Earl, you will have command of *LeFoxxe*. Mr. Anthony will be your second. Mr. Pitts, you will take over the second lieutenant's duties here on *Drakkar*."

Pitts couldn't hide his disappointment. He'd been hoping to get command of one of the schooners. He did manage a "thank you, sir."

"The schooner, *LeCroix*, will be given to Lieutenant Mainard. Sir Lawrence is sending him to us. He was the first lieutenant on one of the brigs that ran aground chasing pirates. It was the admiral's way of saying that no blame should be directed to the young lieutenant for the loss of the brig. The captain was killed when the damned pirates came about and poured a broadside into the brig, even after she had run up on the reef. "No mercy, no quarter." Buck turned to Mr. Markham. "You, young sir, will be Lieutenant Mainard's second. Each ship will have reliable, seasoned hands from *Drakkar* dispersed among its crew. Now, the schooners have been through the prize court, so they're waiting on you to go aboard and take charge. However, it's important that you remember these may only be temporary commands. The Admiralty still has to confirm your appointments, but with Commodore Anthony and Sir Lawrence's recommendations I see no reason the commands will not be confirmed. However, more than one has gone arse hole over tea kettle and lost his command."

This drew smiles and Earl volunteered, "We won't embarrass our new commodore or *Drakkar*, sir. We're very proud of the trust you've placed in us."

"Hear, hear," said the group in unison.

"Now, sirs," Buck started up again, "You have a week to make your ships ready to sail." Buck noticed a hand go up. "Yes, Mr. Davy?"

"Sir, can I hoist the broad pennant?"

Everyone laughed.

Anthony spoke up then, "Of course you can, Mr. Davy, of course you can." He then turned his attentions to the rest of the gathered group. "That about sums it up, gentlemen. Ours is a difficult task, but I know each of you will do his duty."

As the group made its way out of Anthony's quarters, Bart entered. Most of the men spoke a word or two with the wiry cox'n. When Bart had Anthony's eye, he said, "Gigs ready. It's time for your meeting with Commodore Gardner."

Anthony nodded to Bart, and then beckoned to Buck. "I may not be back on board tonight. If I'm delayed as I expect, I'll send Bart back with instructions as to where I can be reached."

As Anthony departed, Buck stared at his back, his mouth agape. "Better close your trap before you choke on flies," the master said jokingly.

Buck closed his mouth and swallowed, "What do you think has got into our commodore?"

"Well, sir, I ain't sure. But were I a betting man, I'd lay odds our commodore has been smitten by that new widow woman."

"Lady Deborah McKean?" Buck asked.

"Aye, sir, that's the one."

***

ANTHONY WAS FIDGETY ALL during his lunch with the commodore. Anticipating his meeting with Lady Deborah, he kept glancing at his watch. Though time seemed to drag on forever, lunch only lasted one hour. Commodore Gardner had proven a jovial host. However, from the start of their meal, it was obvious he was starved for news from England. The commodore quizzed Anthony not only about news from the Admiralty, but he also wanted to hear the latest gossip, rumors, and politics. The meeting did get interesting when the subject of the colonies was brought up. He even appeared to sympathize with the colonies and their cause. When Anthony remarked on his comments the commodore explained.

"Out here we're separated from England. We've come to depend on the colonies for half of our supplies. I'm a personal friend with a number of merchants and shipowners. They've stayed in my house, and I've been a guest in theirs. We've discussed the unfair taxes and trade practices our Parliament has placed upon the Colonials. I've watched as the crown's demands have grown. We've pushed till their backs are against the wall. Oh, I know my duty all right, but I wish Parliament's decisions were made in the boardrooms and not the bedrooms. Damn the French and the Dagos. However, fighting the Colonials is like fighting our friends and neighbors. We'll suffer, Gil. Mark my word...England will suffer."

***

ANTHONY LOOKED UP AS he came down the steps at Government House. Bart was standing there under some palm trees with two horses. He was waiting, but without any degree of enthusiasm. Anthony and Bart had ridden many times, but neither was comfortable on a horse's back. The "note" Anthony had been given by the commodore's wife the previous evening instructed them to use horses rather than a carriage, in that they were less conspicuous. The unsigned note also included a time and a set of directions...nothing further. A signed note could have been damaging and scandalous if it fell into the wrong hands. Nevertheless, Anthony had known the author from the time it was placed in his hand. The anticipated meeting caused both excitement and a touch of caution.

Anthony had never courted a proper "lady." He had had his share of women over the years but they were different, much different. As he and Bart made their way, Anthony took in the view and tranquility of the peaceful island. The sea and the sky seemed to merge. Off in the distance, he could see a small island and Potter's Cay. A gentle wind blew through the palm trees, and birds floated lazily on the air. Anthony and Bart were upon their destination before either realized it. Each had been content to absorb the sun and take in the sights.

The house was more of a summer cottage. It had a large porch that wrapped around three sides. The front room was a large parlor. A breezeway separated the main part of the house from the kitchen and the servant's quarters. A small stable and outbuildings were behind the house.

As Anthony dismounted, Lady Deborah stepped out of the cottage onto the porch. "You can put the horses out back," she said.

Bart took Anthony's horse and questioned, "Do you want me to wait?"

"No," Anthony replied. "It may be a long wait." Bart didn't fail to notice the twinkle in Anthony's eyes as he spoke. Anthony took a couple of guineas from his pocket and gave them to the cox'n. "Enjoy a drink or two before you return to the ship. I'd think it amiss if you made it before the last dog watch."

"Aye, I'll have a wet and maybe a little something extra." Then he was gone.

Turning back to Lady Deborah, Anthony realized that as lovely as the countryside was, it dulled in comparison to the beauty of the woman standing before him. She was wearing a simple gown of emerald green made of a lightweight gauze material. A slight wind blew at her hair and molded the gown to her body, giving ample proof of the woman beneath the cloth. The scene reminded Anthony of a sculpture of a Greek goddess. He felt his breath quicken and blurted, "My God, Lady Deborah. You are beautiful."

Lady Deborah smiled as she reached for his hand and led him into the cottage. "Please," she said, "There must be no formality between us. Let it be Deborah and Gil."

As they sat down for refreshments, Anthony realized Deborah was pouring lemonade for the two of them. That meant she had sent the servants away. After finishing their refreshments

Deborah came over to Anthony's chair.

"You must think me a wanton woman," she said.

"Nonsense," he replied. "You have created in me a feeling I've never felt before. I felt it from the moment you came aboard *Drakkar*. I feel it even more now. You make me feel ...alive. It may be shameless of me, but I have to tell you for the first time in my life, I feel out of control."

"Oh, Gil," she responded, and then she was in his arms. Everything else was a blur. He kissed her...long and passionately. She responded with a hungry kiss of her own. His hand found her breast and she pulled it tight to her. His lips were on her face, neck, and then to her chest and finally her breast.

At some point, he lifted her and carried her into the bedroom. They removed Anthony's uniform, and then he stood dazzled as she dropped her gown to the floor revealing far more than he could have ever imagined.

"Under God's heaven, I've never seen such a lovely sight," he exclaimed.

Their first coupling was frenzied. Both were eager and in need. Afterwards, they lay in each other's arms, both spent from their passion.

"Oh, Gil," Deborah said, as she ran her fingers through the hair on his chest. "I've never known such joy, such pleasure. I feel like a schoolgirl." She rolled over and straddled him.

He playfully ran his hands over her breasts,

teasing them, and then he grasped the hair that hung down on her shoulders and gently pulled her to him so that he could kiss her hardened nipples. Reaching back, she felt his manhood awaken. This time, she guided him into her and began a slow rhythmic motion that brought them to new heights. When the release finally came, she collapsed on him and they slept the contented sleep of lovers.

***

ANTHONY AWOKE AT DAWN and they made love again. As he dressed, Anthony gazed at Deborah as she sat up in bed, her breasts exposed. "Do you know how hard it is for me to leave with you sitting there like that?"

"Obviously not too difficult," she answered, "You continue to dress."

"But not with my usual vigor, my love," he replied, putting on his boots. "When can I see you publicly?"

Deborah took a moment before she responded. "A year is the usual time for mourning, but out here we could get by with six months."

"Six months, damme that is a long time. I want to be with you every minute I can."

Smiling, she said, "You'll have to be content to slip into my bedroom and force your desires on me. Besides," she continued, "it must be kept discreet from all, save Greta."

"Who is Greta?" interrupted Anthony.

"The commodore's wife," Deborah explained.

He was right. They were confidants.

"Anyway," Deborah continued again, "Greta tells me you're getting *Drakkar* and those little ships ready and will be sailing soon."

Anthony nodded. He suddenly felt depressed at the thought of leaving Deborah so soon after he'd found her.

Sensing his mood, Deborah left the bed and came to him. He hugged her close, feeling her bosom and stomach drawn tightly against him. Their kiss was long and loving.

Deborah could feel the roughness of his uniform against her body. She could make out the faint odor of tar mixed with salt. These were odors of her sailor, her love.

"Don't worry, my darling," she said, "I'll always be here waiting when you return."

PART II

Spell of the Deep
What magic spells does the sea
Cast upon a man
To sail away from all he loves
It's hard to understand
Fearing not the wind and wave
The deep that has no sound
The captain walks his quarterdeck
A ship that's fit-n-sound

...Michael Aye

Chapter Eight

THE WIND HAD BACKED to the southwest. *Drakkar* had every inch of canvas spread and was laid close to the centerline, yet she clawed for every yard. The two schooners appeared to be making a better time of it. This is what they were rigged for. They were built for speed, like greyhounds on the ocean. However, their light, fragile hulls made them more vulnerable to gunfire if they couldn't escape to windward. A schooner had two masts with two equal sized mainsails, gaff-rigged and extended by booms. The topsails were square-rigged with a square mainsail. Anthony had heard the master commenting to young Davy about what a sight they made under full canvas.

"Fine sight 'eh lad? I'll give it to the Colonials. They knows how to make a fine ship."

"Colonials made those ships?" Davy asked. "But they have French names."

"Aye, lad. Schooners are a product of North America. Just as the cutter was made for the coast off our Kent and Sussex."

Looking at the schooners, Anthony thought of

Gabe. He could imagine how he and Lieutenant Earl were enjoying their freedom, being out from under the "commodore."

"Deck there," the masthead lookout called down. "*LeFoxxe* is signaling."

"Ship, nay two ships, off the larboard bow."

Anthony turned and saw Buck with a glass to his eye.

"Acknowledge," Anthony said. "Have them investigate but not engage if it's a superior force."

"Mr. Davy."

"Yes, sir."

"Take a glass and go aloft. Let me know as soon as we are in sight of the two vessels."

"Aye, sir." Up the ratlines the youth went, his energy and desire to please not lost on Anthony. A few minutes later, Davy shouted down, "Two ships lying to, sir."

Buck rolled his eyes and muttered, "Gawd have mercy!"

"Can you be more definitive, Mr. Davy?" Anthony called up, trying not to laugh at Buck's frustrated comment. He knew the regular lookout, a seasoned sailor, could have called down the sighting, but Anthony wanted Mr. Davy to get the experience.

"Deck there," Davy shouted again. "One is a merchant ship, sir. The other appears to be a schooner. She's square-rigged and is much like *LeFoxxe*. The schooner must have seen *LeFoxxe*, sir. She's getting underway."

"Deck there." This time it was the regular lookout. "She be a pirate, sir. She's fired on *LeFoxxe*."

Anthony turned to Buck, "Beat to quarters."

"Aye, sir."

Over the sound of bosun pipes and drum beats, the masthead lookout called down again. "The schooner looks like she's trying to run to starboard, but the merchant ship is still laying hove to and in 'er way. *LeFoxxe* 'as fired 'er broadside and scored several hits." This time there was excitement in the lookout's voice, "I saw several bits and pieces flying before the smoke blocked me view. She's coming outta the smoke now, sir," the lookout continued, "and it looks like she's a couple more points to starboard."

Anthony and Buck looked at each other upon hearing this. "Trapped like the rat she is," exclaimed Buck.

Anthony nodded and ordered, "Signal *LeCroix* to engage the enemy."

"*LeCroix* has acknowledged," Davy called down, still at the masthead.

"Think she'll fight or run?" asked Peckham.

"What would you do?" Anthony answered the master.

"Aye, it's a hanging if they're captured," the master replied.

Anthony called to the bosun, "Give Mr. Pitts my compliments and tell him I'd like to see him as soon as he can turn over his duties to the gunner."

"Aye, sir."

When Pitts arrived he was breathless. He was obviously anticipating Anthony's summons by the speed at which he arrived.

"Damme, Mr. Pitts," exclaimed Anthony. "I've not seen one so eager to knock on St. Peter's door."

Smiling, Pitts responded, "No guts, no glory, sir."

"Well have a care, sir. The men with you might not be so anxious. Now, if you can control yourself, muster a boarding party forward with the bosun. My compliments to Lieutenant Dunn. Have him loan you a squad of marines to go with your boarding party. Then ask him to attend me, please."

"Aye, sir." Pitts answered as he rushed off.

There was now no more than a mile between the converging ships. From above, the lookout called down again, "The chase 'as tacked, sir."

"Thinks he'll make for some inlet and lose us'ns," the master opined to the helmsman.

"Sir," Lieutenant Dunn said, announcing his arrival.

"Yes, Lieutenant Dunn," Anthony said. "I would appreciate it, sir, if you would post your best sharpshooters in the rigging as soon as you think proper."

"Directly, sir," Lieutenant Dunn replied as he dashed off.

The three ships, *Drakkar*, *LeFoxxe*, and *LeCroix*

now formed a triangle with the chase in the middle with nowhere to go. "The rogue's let loose a broadside," Buck volunteered.

"Pop guns," snorted the master.

Anthony had his glass to his eye, but replied to the master's comment. "Pop guns they may be, but damnable accurate." He had seen through his glass jagged, gaping holes along *LeFoxxe's* bulwark where she had been hit.

LeFoxxe and *LeCroix* were both returning fire and their accuracy was not without merit. "They've hit her good," Buck exclaimed. "There goes her mainmast."

"I bet that took the wind outer her," said the master, chuckling at this pun.

LeFoxxe and *LeCroix* were now grappling with the schooner, one larboard and the other starboard.

Anthony turned to the master, "Bring her up a couple points and put us across her stern so we can board aft."

"Aye," the master replied and barked his orders to the quartermaster. The distance was now less than a cable.

Lieutenant Pitts called to his men, "Boarders make ready." The bosun was there checking each man's weapons. Some had cutlasses and pikes while others had tomahawks. Some were even armed with service pistols.

Bart looked at Anthony and casually commented, "I 'ope that pistol don't go off accidental like. Way it's pointing it'd change yer love life substantial like, I'm thinking."

Anthony looked down. Bart had helped buckle on his sword, but handed him his pistol. When he'd stuck the pistol in his waistband he'd inadvertently cocked his pistol. Now he had a loaded, cocked pistol pointed toward his manhood.

"You vulgar dog," Anthony said, quickly easing the hammer down to the half-cocked position.

"Nay, Cap'n," Bart said, still calling Anthony cap'n and not commodore. "Just looking out for the lady's interest."

Anthony then remembered Davy was still aloft. "Mr. Davy, bring yourself down if you please and take station by the master."

"Aye, sir," Davy replied. Then grinning, he came sliding down the backstay with such speed it startled Anthony. Gone was the timid boy who had reported on board a few months back. Davy was now a seasoned midshipman.

Drakkar groaned as she touched with the schooner. "Boarders away, boarders away." Mr. Pitts and his group poured over onto the smaller ship, cutting down all resistance as they went. Lieutenant Dunn's marine sharpshooters were making their presence felt as well.

A torrent of curses and groans, some English and some in French came from every quarter. Musket and pistol shots filled the air, the smoke from the shots leaving a pungent odor that burnt the eyes and nostrils. *Clang-clang* — metal on metal as cutlass encountered cutlass, bright metal turning dark from blood and gore.

"To me," Buck screamed as he deflected a boarding pike, and then with a quick maneuver slashed at the man attacking him. The slash opened up the man's belly, spilling his innards onto the deck. Mercifully, one of *Drakkar's* marines shot the man, ending his agony.

As Anthony stepped over a body, a man jumped up from behind one of the cannons and with a savage laugh attacked him. The attack was over before it began as Mr. Pitts quickly shot the man with his pistol.

Holding the smoking pistol, he calmly volunteered, "Sounded like a bloody maniac, Captain."

Drakkar's crew continued to surge forward against the pirates. However, like madmen, they continued to fight and die.

Gabe and Earl found themselves back to back, fending off two attackers. One of the rogues struck a heavy blow that felled Earl, leaving Gabe to protect his friend and fend for himself. At this moment Dagan came into view. Seeing Gabe's predicament created a sense of urgency in Dagan. He attacked the foe before him with such savagery that Lord Anthony almost felt sorrow for the fellow. The brute lunged at Dagan, who deflected the other's cutlass. Then with a ferocious blow, he completely beheaded the man. Dispatching this opponent brought Dagan to Gabe's side, who was still fending off the two attackers at once. Dagan's blade was a large broadsword. His next swing caused the heavy blade to completely sever his opponent's arm. It fell to the deck lifeless, its fingers still clutching the hilt of his blade. The wounded fellow was in shock, looking at the stump that a moment ago had been his arm. As blood spurted from severed arteries, the man turned white and then collapsed, dead before he hit the deck.

The overwhelming numbers from *Drakkar* and her consorts soon overran all resistance. One of the survivors was a man in a filthy uniform coat of a French naval lieutenant. He had laid down his weapons and cried for mercy. Gabe pointed at the red flag still flying aloft and shouted, "You dare beg for mercy while flying the red flag?" He spat in disgust and turned his attention to Lieutenant Earl. Anthony walked up just as Gabe helped Earl to his feet.

Earl reached up and touched the side of his head. Blood had started to congeal, but when he touched his head it started to ooze again. Wincing as he touched the nasty cut, Earl pulled his bloody hand away.

Gabe snickered at the sight. "Damme, Stephen. The rogue has lopped off the top of your ear. I hope your hat still fits."

Earl looked at Gabe and said, "Aye, but for you he'd have had my whole damn head."

Dunn's marines, along with a few of the hands from the boarding party, had rounded up the last of the surviving pirates. The dead ones were unceremoniously tossed over the side. "Give the sharks a bellyache," Bart had said. Anthony also noticed, but chose to ignore, that the dead pirates were being relieved of anything of value prior to becoming shark bait.

A thorough search was made of the ship, resulting in Mr. Markham's find. "Sir, we've found some very official looking papers. They're written in French. There's also a small chest with specie and one with a few gems and the like, such as a lady would wear."

Anthony followed Markham down to the pirate captain's cabin and was surprised but glad to see the midshipman had taken the initiative to put a marine guard at the door. There were several letters as Markham had mentioned. Anthony could only make out a few words here and there as the letters were soiled with food and drink; however, one letter appeared to be talking about a fifty-gun frigate. It also contained a page that was better cared for than the rest and it was filled with dates in one column and numbers in another column.

Markham volunteered, "It appears like code, sir, for a rendezvous on certain dates-but where? I think the number represents a location." Anthony agreed with Markham's assessment.

"Look here, sir," Markham had picked up another paper. At the top was the word "*Reaper.*" Under one column was 27-28 June and across from it in another column the single digit "six." A very valuable clue and a very simple code, but without more information it would be impossible to break.

Anthony turned to a bosun's mate who was close by. "My compliments to Lieutenant Dunn. Ask him to have that French speaking prisoner in the navy coat taken over to *Drakkar* and held by the mainmast."

"Aye, sir," the sailor replied and then was gone.

"Do you speak French, Mr. Markham?" Anthony asked.

"Only a little, sir."

"It will have to do. I don't want the prisoner to know that I do, so you will act as my interpreter."

"Aye, sir."

Once Anthony and his accompanying officers got back on *Drakkar*. he found Lieutenant Dunn had the pirate trussed up and under guard.

"Mr. Buck."

"Aye, sir."

"Assemble the crew to witness punishment."

Buck looked at Anthony somewhat bewildered. "Punishment, sir?"

"Yes, Mr. Buck, a hanging," Anthony replied, certain that the French pirate understood more English than he let on. Well he could think on that.

"A hanging, sir?" Buck questioned.

"Yes, dammit, a hanging," Anthony snapped. "Here or Antigua makes no difference. His fate was sealed when they attacked the merchant-man. Lieutenant Mainard!"

"Yes sir," Mainard replied. He was pondering the pirate's hanging when his name was called suddenly.

"Loosen your grapnels and go check on the vessel the rogues were having at, and take the surgeon with you."

"Aye, sir." Mainard left to do his bidding, somewhat relieved that he was being sent on an errand and wouldn't have to witness the hanging.

Anthony then turned back to Buck, "Carry on with the business at hand."

"Yes sir," was all Buck could manage. The order was given and the drums started to roll. A rope was thrown over the yardarm, a hangman's noose already fashioned at the end of it.

The pirate collapsed into a heap on the deck. Two of Dunn's marines were trying to lift the whimpering man but he refused to stand. Anthony nodded and the marines let go. The prisoner hit the deck with a thud.

"S'il-vous-plait, monsieur!" the pathetic man begged, reaching out with his arm to Anthony. Tears streamed down his face causing streaks in the grime from the recent battle.

"Donnez moi une chance," he cried. The man's actions were disgusting to the hardened sailors who had seen the red flag flying from the pirate's mast, not to mention the torn and mutilated bodies the pirates had left in their wake. The cries for mercy fell on deaf ears.

"Gawd 'e makes me sick to me stomach," a voice in the crowd spoke as the pirate whimpered and crawled in a semi circle.

"Hang the bugger, Cap'n," another voice in the crowd said.

"Silence!" Buck ordered.

Anthony, Buck, Gabe, and Lieutenant Dunn all stood before the man. The marines continued to hold him up as Anthony spoke to him. "Do you understand English?"

"Oui, monsieur."

"Are you a French officer?"

"Non, monsieur."

"Why are you wearing a French naval officer's coat then?"

"It was, how do you say....plunder." He muttered some more comments, which couldn't be understood.

Markham volunteered, "I think he's trying to tell us he took it from someone's things after the man had been killed."

Still not letting on he could understand the man's pleas, Anthony spoke to Markham, "Well, tell him I think he's a lying son of a cur dog, and that I'm holding him responsible for that ship over there." He pointed to the ship that had been the pirate's prey.

"Tell him he's been caught in the act of piracy. There's no doubt of his guilt and the penalty is death."

The Frenchman understood enough of what was said such that he'd started his begging and pleading even before Markham could translate.

Disgusted, Anthony ordered, "String him up!"

Lieutenant Dunn nodded to his sergeant who stepped forward, placed the noose around the pirate's neck, and tightened it. Once the sergeant was satisfied, he stepped back and looked at Lieutenant Dunn, who in turn looked to Anthony.

Anthony nodded and Lieutenant Dunn ordered, "Haul him up." A group of marines started pulling on the rope. The French pirate's cries were cut off as the rope bit into the flesh, cutting off the man's air. As he was lifted off the deck, his feet started kicking in the air and his body started to sway. The onlookers were stoic. Most had never witnessed a hanging and were aghast.

"Avast, hauling, let him down," Anthony ordered. The rope was turned loose and the pirate thudded as he hit the deck, gasping for air. The marine sergeant loosened the noose and the pirate started to breathe.

Anthony looked at Markham, "Tell him that was my only warning. Next time, he'll hang till the gulls have pecked his eyes out." Markham repeated Anthony's comments.

"Now ask him who commanded his vessel."

The pirate answered quickly, "Capitaine Allemand."

"Where is he now?"

"Dead. He was shot as your men boarded."

"Is the *Reaper* a French ship...a frigate?"

"She is big but not as big as some. She is similar to this ship and she has fifty cannons. Her capitaine is French like I am."

"But is the ship French?" The pirate shrugged and stated, "She flies no flag. The men answer only to Capitaine Jabot."

"When were you to rendezvous with the *Reaper*?"

The pirate looked frightened and could only shrug. Angered, Anthony ordered, "Haul him up."

"Please," the man begged before the noose could tighten. "Only Capitaine Allemand knew. He kept his papers locked up and no one else knew what they contained. Please, Monsieur."

After further questioning, Anthony found out the man had signed on at Martinique a few months back. However, no more useful information could be gained.

His was a damned difficult job. From Falmouth to Barbados was forty-two hundred miles, and near about that many from Jamaica to Falmouth. A lot of ocean to cover. However, it seemed that all the attacks were taking place within a day's sailing from islands of the West Indies. This seemed to narrow it down. But what did this mean? They would need bases to supply themselves and to trade their ill-gotten goods. Did they also have a spy at these locations? The key had to be the rendezvous areas. Yet without solving that puzzle it all depended on luck.

***

LeCROIX HAD CLOSED WITH the merchant vessel. She was a small snow with a crew of mostly islanders. The pirates had turned everything upside down. Most of the officers and crew had been killed and tossed overboard by the pirates. Sharks were in frenzy around the helpless ship. The surgeon reported to Anthony, "Nothing much for me to do. Work for a chaplain maybe, but not for me."

Lieutenant Mainard reported aboard *Drakkar*. "Papers say she's outta St. Lucia, sir. With a name cross her stern like 'New Haven' I would assume she belongs to a colonial."

"I agree," Anthony said. "Is she ready to sail?"

"Aye, sir. The pirates were out for blood, not for destroying the ship."

"We'll leave her surviving crew on board. They'll be more comfortable there than on *Drakkar*. Mr. Buck!"

"Aye, sir."

"Put Gabe with a good master's mate on board the snow and supplement its crew with a few of our men. He can take her back to English Harbour."

"Aye, sir," Buck said, then hesitated. "I er..., I thought I'd put Lieutenant Pitts on the *Rascal*."

Anthony frowned, "*Rascal*!"

"Aye, sir. That's the name of the schooner, the pirate's vessel."

"Oh yes," Anthony answered, aggravated at his dullness. Trying to cover he said, "It'll make Pitts' dreams come true. You've likely doomed us all, Mr. Buck."

Buck look puzzled, "How so, sir?"

Anthony smiled and replied, "Now that he's got a taste of command, there'll be no stopping Pitts. I'm sure he'll make admiral before we do, as the master once predicted."

Laughing, Buck said, "That could be, sir, that could be."

The return trip to Antigua was uneventful. One coastal vessel had been spotted, but before Buck could call "hands to braces" it had scattered to a nearby island. Approaching English Harbour, Anthony could only guess at the impression the group would make as they headed toward their anchorage.

Drakkar had departed with the two schooners. Now instead of the three ships that Anthony had sailed with, he was entering the harbour with five. This would surely cause a stir. Breaking his reverie, the master called out to no one in particular, "Flagship is gone."

Commodore Gardner was now the senior naval officer on station and Anthony was second. *What a difference a few days made*, Anthony thought. But his mind kept drifting to a little cottage on a hill and Lady Deborah.

Clearing his mind from the thoughts of his woman, Anthony realized several ships were at anchor that had not been present when *Drakkar* had sailed. A sloop of war, a brig, and the mail packet were all lying at anchor. The flagship was gone, as the master had said. The captains of the new ships were taking advantage of the flagship having sailed. They were, no doubt, taking the time to enjoy the simple pleasures of the island, causing a pang of jealously in Anthony that he found surprising.

Chapter Nine

For the next several months things were quiet. Anthony was able to keep the schooner *Rascal* after she was "bought in," but the snow was sent to England. Lieutenant Pitts was left in command of *Rascal*, but he knew it was only temporary. Anthony was able to sign on most of the snow's surviving hands. He was a little concerned about how the crew would react to the islanders. He'd never had a Negro on board his ship before. However, his concerns were for naught. The crew accepted the blacks well enough. They had been divided into two groups-the larger on board *Rascal*, and the other smaller group on *LeCroix*.

Anthony had also divided his squadron of "terriers", as the master was so fond of calling them, into two groups. *LeFoxxe* and *LeCroix* went out in pairs. That way Pitts, being less experienced, would be under *Drakkar's* watchful eye. By dividing his command into pairs, he could maintain a degree of safety and still patrol a greater area than would be possible if *Drakkar* was a lone ship. The pickings had been slim, however. Anthony enjoyed his forays ashore with Lady Deborah, but felt a growing need to be at sea. Out there he could possibly meet up with the *Reaper*, and put an end to the devil's reign of terror. During one patrol, Lieutenant Pitt's crew had picked up a poor man who had survived by clinging to a hatch cover after his ship was destroyed. The fellow was about done in from thirst, and half cooked by the sun. In his delirium, the man spoke of a great black ship with matching stygian sails. "The ship just came out of the dawn," he said. The poor soul cried when he described how the ship was looted. To make for a more sinister situation, the pirates carried two screaming lady passengers away. He explained that after taking everything of value, the devil ship cast off, and then fired a whole broadside, completely destroying the little merchant ship.

Commodore Gardner had told Anthony that messages of lost or missing ships continued to trickle in. The schooners had picked up a couple of smaller coastal vessels for piracy. Lieutenant Pitts, on the schooner *Rascal*, had made the last capture. But all in all, their work was futile, creating a greater sense of urgency and frustration for Anthony.

"The season is upon us," explained Commodore Gardner. "Nobody wants to be caught in a hurricane, be he merchant or rogue. Therefore, there should be a break in the devilment."

Anthony's little flotilla found out first hand what the commodore had meant in late August.

They had just rendezvoused off the windward island of St. Vincent on the Caribbean side when the storm began. Suddenly, the sea had become a deadly foe, as much an enemy as the pirates they were trying to apprehend. The master cursed as he was summoned from the wardroom by a concerned watch. However, the curse died on his lips as the storm had turned into a full gale. A master's mate was already lashing down one of the helmsmen so he wouldn't be washed overboard.

The master hurried to help lash down the other helmsman. "Four men-we need four men at the wheel to keep control," Peckham ordered his mate, noting the captain was now on deck, followed by the first lieutenant.

The wind whipped the waves as they came crashing down over the bow, sending rivers of water surging down the deck, tearing at everything in their path. No sooner had one watch been dismissed before all hands were called to shorten sail or take down torn canvas. Anthony remained on deck during the entire ordeal. He had on his oilskins but was drenched, and due to the wind, somewhat chilled. He couldn't help but worry not only about *Drakkar*, but also of Gabe and the others on the more fragile schooners.

The waves continued to crash against *Drakkar's* thick hull. The ship groaned as it fought its way through the raging waters. Lightning lit up the sky in great flashes. The wind howled, and caused the shrouds and stays to fairly sing. Anthony blinked, trying to clear the stinging salt spray from his eyes.

Buck had been helping to free a blocked tackle when he lost his footing and was knocked into the scuppers as the raging water sluiced down the larboard side. He found himself being hauled unceremoniously to his feet as huge hands grabbed the neck of his slicker and jerked him from the cascading torrent, setting him upright on deck.

McMorgan, the burly bosun, had been his rescuer. "Got 'ya trained now sir, so I don't want to lose 'ya and have to train another," the big man had explained, smiling as he did so.

Buck, bruised and half drowned, muttered, "Glad to hear you feel so, bosun. Right glad I am to hear it."

Anthony grew more concerned about the schooners. The seas were getting big and he was fearful of a rogue wave catching one of the fragile ships on one quarter and broaching her. The wind continued to increase, and instead of coming from directly astern as it had been, it seemed to come from all directions.

"Can you see the schooners?" Peckham asked. The old master was unshaven and hollow-eyed. Even with his rotund belly, he looked gaunt. Peering aft beyond the turbulent waves, one of the schooners could be seen. But which one?

"She's taken in everything but the foresail," Buck yelled to make himself heard above the wind.

"Aye," Peckham agreed. "She looks like she may over reach us under bare sticks."

The avalanche of water continued to crash against *Drakkar's* bow, making the ship shudder and creating terror in the crew. They responded when called, but fighting the storm sapped a man's strength, making each maneuver a life or death struggle.

MacMorgan could barely see, the wind stinging his eyes, as he reported to Anthony. "One of the forward cannons has tried to break away from its lashings, Cap'n, but we's doubled up on 'em so's she's not likely to come adrift. There's two feet or more o' water in the well but I got crews on the pumps and the water don't appear to be gaining. I've taken me mates and checked below the waterline and so far we's not sprung a plank!"

The news was good but they were not out of trouble yet. On and on until it seemed like forever. Waves grew bigger and bigger, until they looked mountainous.

"Looks to me to be a mountain," Bart had sworn, "I never seen such a storm."

"It's a hurricane," Peckham exclaimed. "This ain't no gale, it's a hurricane."

They had run all the way to Jamaica before the hurricane had veered northerly toward Cuba. The black sky began to turn gray and then clear even more. The sharp rain that had pelted the watch like tiny daggers slowed and then stopped.

The surging sea that had tossed *Drakkar* around like a twig grew less angry and was now only fast rolling swells. Anxious men were now giving a sigh of relief, having survived more than they thought they could. They had been lucky, very lucky. Sails were torn. Rigging was damaged and cordage was everywhere. One of the ship's boats had been smashed. All this was superficial. *Drakkar* was afloat. They had survived.

Bart had summed up Anthony's feelings exactly in a comment he made to Silas. "Glad I am that's over. I ain't yet ready to cast me lot with old King Neptune. Not yet I ain't."

Chapter Ten

GABE AND MARKHAM HAD each turned eighteen, and both were now ready to sit for the lieutenant's exam. They each had birthdays in November, Gabe's on the thirteenth and Markham's on the nineteenth. They shared much more than a birth month: both had mischievous natures. Anthony had been relieved that most of their pranks had been carried out ashore and neither had required discipline from the bosun.

Lady Deborah had decided to give a birthday party for the two "middies." She had invited every young lady on the island, all of whom showed up for the festivities in their finest attire, each trying to out-do the other for the young gentlemen's attention. Lieutenant Earl was present also. He and Gabe entertained the young ladies with their musical abilities to the delight of all. Lord Anthony was thankful that they'd kept it clean, unlike the lewd pieces they played on board ship.

Gabe and Markham had become close friends, and were well-liked by the other officers under Anthony's command. The two young gentlemen had grown not only in stature, but as responsible officers as well. It was hard to think of the two as mids, they had matured so much since the commission had started. Anthony was certain both would pass the exam. The only problem was having enough post captains in port at one time to form a board. With the holidays rapidly approaching, surely a couple of ships with post captains would arrive.

Anthony heard the sound of laughter and a feminine giggle. The gentlemen seemed to be well occupied by the flirting young ladies, leaving Anthony with the feeling that the furthest thing from Gabe and Markham's minds was the lieutenant's exam.

***

NEW YEAR'S DAY IN the year of our Lord 1775 found Lady Deborah a guest aboard *Drakkar*, along with Commodore Gardner and his wife, Greta. Also on board for the festivities were Captain Swift and Captain Meade. Captain Swift was in command of *HMS Roebuck*, a new forty-four gun frigate that was barely a year old. Captain Meade commanded the *Magic* frigate of thirty-two guns. Both were on convoy duty from Portsmouth. Anthony was very excited that the two captains were on station. It would probably take weeks for the convoy to be assembled for the trip back to England. During that time, with Commodore Gardner's help, a board could be convened for the lieutenant's exam.

After completing one of the finest meals Silas had ever prepared, cigars were passed around, and those who preferred pipes lit them. Lady Deborah and Greta excused themselves to the upper deck where Lieutenant Earl and Gabe were entertaining the crew with their music during this festive time. A few of the crew joined in the merriment. Bart carried chairs up for the ladies.

A warm greeting to the men by the ladies and a sharp scowl from Bart ensured there would be no profane language or vulgar comments while the ladies were on deck. "Watch ye words or ye'll answer to me," Bart threatened.

Meanwhile, back in Anthony's quarters, Silas was pouring claret for everyone. When the glasses were filled, Anthony broached the subject of an examination board. He was somewhat surprised at how quickly the captains agreed to convene a board. It appeared both captains had mids that were ready for the exam as well. In fact, Captain Meade had two. "One's past his prime and the other is just now ripe," he explained.

Upon the approval of Commodore Gardner, as senior naval officer of Antigua, a board was scheduled for the lieutenant's exam to be held the following Wednesday. That would be the first Wednesday of the month. As luck would have it, two brigs, a sloop of war, and a frigate all dropped anchor within the next few days. The frigate was the captured French ship, the *Tyger*. She was small, a sixth rate, but was commanded by a post captain. This resulted in there now being three post captains in port to sit on the board with Commodore Gardner as the President.

Gabe and Markham had been called to Lord Anthony's cabin and told the board was being convened. The two busied themselves getting all their papers together and going over some last minute questions with the master. Only a week ago there had been just a handful of midshipmen on the island. Therefore, Gabe and Markham had been somewhat in demand in regards to the island's social scene. Both young gentlemen were at the top of the list to receive invitations from various young ladies. The two had basked in their celebrity, but now there seemed to be midshipmen everywhere. All were acting as important as admirals.

"The only good thing about all these shit-souled younkers coming out of the woodwork, is that the board is bound to recognize the only two real seamen in the lot," offered Markham.

"Aye," Gabe answered, "But if the little turds anger the board, it will go hard on us all."

Markham nodded, seeing the logic in Gabe's comments. "Well, if they do I'll keelhaul me a little bastard and that's no idle promise."

Gabe couldn't help but laugh; such was the vehemence in his friend's comments. "Let's go have a wet and cool your humours."

***

"It's a shit pot load," Markham exclaimed to Gabe as they approached Government House for the lieutenant's exam. A large group had already gathered. Some were in little two or three men groups with texts out, asking each other questions. Others were nervously pacing, and one was obviously the worse for drink. Once, when a question was being asked in one of the little groups, Gabe and Markham overheard both the question and answer. Looking to his friend, Gabe declared, "I knew that"-to which Markham replied somewhat sarcastically, "Of course," not trying to hide his disbelief. Gabe counted thirteen mids for the exam. Thirteen! Of all the bad luck.

"Damn, there are thirteen of us," Gabe told Markham. "Why couldn't it have been twelve or fourteen?" Gabe had never been superstitious, but this just seemed an omen.

At 8 A.M., a stooped, gray-haired little clerk from the commodore's staff opened the front door. A hush fell over the group of assembled young gentlemen. Gabe began to feel more nervous. What if he failed? He didn't want to let his brother down, or his dead father for that matter. "What'd you expect from the bastard?" some would say. His stomach growled and he felt Markham punch him. The punch broke Gabe's train of thought, and he realized the clerk was speaking.

"Now, young sirs, make sure you have all your documents and bonifides ready and in good order. There's no time to return to your ship to fetch some certificates left behind." The clerk sounded like a schoolteacher. "Now, sirs, so as to maintain proper discipline and good order, we will proceed according to the alphabet."

Gabe turned to Markham and said, "Hell's fire." As Gabe turned away, Markham pleaded, "Don't make 'em mad, Gabe. Please don't anger 'em."

When Gabe entered the boardroom the commodore greeted him. "Ah, Mr. Anthony, your packet please."

Absently, Anthony handed his packet to the captain sitting by the commodore. There was a single chair sitting in front of the long table where the examining board was seated.

"Would you care to sit down, sir?"

"Oh, no sir," Gabe responded, trying to focus, trying to get his senses about him.

"Mr. Anthony, let me introduce you to the board," said the commodore. "At the far end of the table on my left is Captain Williams from *Tyger*, next is Captain Meade of *Magic*, and to my right is Captain Swift of *Roebuck*." Each officer had nodded his greeting.

Captain Swift started things off. "I see you've seen considerable action for one so young. I also see your father was an admiral, and your brother has raised his broad pennant!"

"Yes sir," Gabe stoically replied.

"Do you expect any favors from this board because of your relations being senior officers?"

"No, sir!"

"Good," replied Swift in a harsh voice, "Cause there'll be none."

Oh, shit, thought Gabe.

Next Captain Meade said, "Tell me about some of those actions against the pirates you encountered."

After telling of the actions with the pirates, and the prizes that they had taken, Gabe started to relax. He was asked a few questions about strategy and what he'd change if given the opportunity. Gabe was gaining confidence when the commodore announced, "Well, enough of that, shall we proceed."

Gabe felt the wind sucked from his sails. Each captain seemed to have his own little pet niche and Gabe was bombarded with questions regarding these particular niches. He was sweating, feeling thirsty and somewhat dizzy when the commodore said, "I've no further questions."

At first, Gabe didn't comprehend the commodore's comment. His eyes were stinging from sweat dripping in them. His shirt was damp and clung to him from the perspiration, but he managed to find a dry spot on the cuff and wipe his eyes. The commodore was in counsel with the captains. When he turned around, he stuck out his hand to Gabe.

"I'm pleased to announce that it's the opinion of this board that you've shown the knowledge, leadership, and competency expected. Therefore, you have been passed for lieutenancy."

A sigh of relief escaped Gabe. Captain Swift, who was now smiling for the first time, shook Gabe's hand and then stated, "Now, run tell your brother the good news."

"Thank you, sir. Thank all of you," Gabe replied, excitedly.

***

Markham was waiting when Gabe came out. "You didn't bugger it for us, did you?" Ignoring Markham's comments, Gabe blurted out, "I passed, I bloody passed!" Several of the waiting mids glared at Gabe. He didn't care. He'd passed!

"Damn," Markham said smiling. He was happy for his friend. "You were in there forever. How was it?"

"Hush," the clerk scolded. Looking at Gabe, he said, "Be off with you, young sir."

"Gotta go," Gabe told Markham. "We'll meet later."

Chapter Eleven

DAGAN AND BART WERE at the jetty waiting when Gabe arrived. "I passed!" Gabe shouted jubilantly.

"He don't look like no ossifer to me," joked Bart.

"If he is, he's poorly dressed," Dagan added, and then asked, "Did they dunk you boy? You look fairly drenched." Gabe ignored the two and made his way into the boat.

Bart then turned to the boatmen, "Look alive, we got us a new ossifer."

Several of the men smiled and a few snickered good-naturedly as the boat cast off from the jetty.

"Have 'is own ship soon, like as not," volunteered Dawkins, the old seaman who Gabe had saved from having his leg crushed in a gun drill several months ago. "I'd serve 'im, I would," he said, and all agreed with the old salt's sentiment.

As the ship's boat approached *Drakkar*, the sentry called out, "Boat ahoy!"

"Aye, aye." Bart's reply to the challenge said it all. An officer had returned to come aboard his ship.

Anthony and Buck were waiting for Gabe at the quarterdeck. After congratulations were given, Anthony looked at his brother and was proud of what he saw.

"Let's go down to my cabin for refreshment," Anthony said, putting his arm across his brother's shoulder as they went down to his quarters.

Upon entering the cabin, Anthony called to Silas, "Fetch us a bottle of hock then be off with you." When Silas left, Anthony looked at Gabe and said, "Father would have been very proud of you, as I am. Now tell me about it."

Markham returned an hour or so later in just as jubilant a mood. He too had passed and was heartily congratulated as Gabe had been. Anthony planned a dinner that evening to celebrate Gabe and Markham's passing the lieutenant's exam. All the officers in Anthony's squadron were invited. Gabe and Markham were both very pleased that the commodore was honoring them. However, the celebration was for passing the exam only; that was only the first part. They still had to receive their commissions. Until that time they were still midshipmen. Buck called to the two as Gabe and Markham were heading to change into their work uniforms.

"I hear that of the thirteen mids who went before the board only six were passed." This was indeed news to the young gentlemen.

"Less than half," Markham stated.

"Aye," Gabe answered but added, "That means less competition for any available commissions."

As the two departed *Drakkar* for *LeFoxxe* and *LeCroix*, Gabe recalled Captain Swift's remarks about special consideration being given due to who his relatives were. The good captain had to say publicly what was considered politically correct. Yet in Gabe's mind he was sure connection played a big part in promotions. He hoped a deserving candidate was not passed over just so somebody's lackey could be promoted. Gabe was sure of his own abilities, and of Markham's. But he couldn't help but think of Witzenfeld. Witz should have never been made lieutenant. Witzenfeld's promotion was in itself proof he had patronage and special interest at some high level. Would his past difficulties with Witz come to haunt him at some point in the future? *I shall keep a weather eye*, Gabe promised himself.

Suddenly Gabe felt a swat to the back of his head. Turning quickly, he faced Markham, who had his hat in his hand.

"You ain't been listening to a word I have said, have you?" Markham asked.

Realizing he'd tuned Markham out, but not meaning to be rude to his friend, Gabe replied, "I'm sorry, I was lost in thought."

"Huh," snorted Markham. "I was saying, I bet that snot-nosed, carrot-headed shit on Commodore Gardner's staff is sure to get a commission while his betters have to wait."

Gabe had to laugh. Markham was never one to hide his feelings. His particular dislike of the young gentleman in question had more to do with his being stationed ashore and more readily available to entertain a certain young lady. Carrot-head's assignment to the dockyard meant most nights were free, while Markham was frequently at sea for days on end.

***

THE DINNER THAT NIGHT was a feast. Plenty of good-natured ribbing went on, and toasts were made. As the evening drew to a close, Anthony stood and tapped on a wineglass to quiet the officers before him. Once he had their attention, he called to the first lieutenant. "Mr. Buck, did you not tell me we had some important news arrive this evening that will certainly affect the daily operation of *Drakkar*?"

"Aye sir, that's true, it is," replied Buck. "The guard boat has brought us these two letters I hold in my hand. One is addressed to Lieutenant Gabriel Anthony, Esquire; and the other is to Lieutenant Frances Markham, Esquire. Now unless I'm mistaken, I'd bet these official looking packets are commissions." When Buck handed the lieutenants their commissions, Anthony stood again.

"Gentlemen, a toast to our two new lieutenants." This started the merriment all over again.

Dagan, Bart, and the bosun were all standing aft enjoying their pipes and a wee touch of rum themselves.

"Sounds like a proper wetting down, don't it?" the bosun said, commenting on the noise coming through the open transom windows and the skylight.

"Aye," Dagan responded, "Think of all the pounding heads tomorrow."

"Sure nuff," Bart agreed, "Likely we'll have to see things are done proper till noon. I can't see any of them being clear-headed before then."

"Aye," they all agreed, turning their attention to the rum at hand.

***

WITH THE HOLIDAYS ENDING, the pirates started attacking more frequently. Ships were looted and then destroyed with only a rare survivor to tell the tale. More often it was a piece of wreckage or flotsam that told the story. Thus far there had been no captives held for ransom. This lone fact made Anthony suspicious. Typically, pirates would be more than willing to hold a captive for ransom if there were any money to be had. There had to be some connections, else why turn down sure money? The pirates were not fools. There had to be a reason why no one had been offered up for ransom. Was it fear of being recognized? Was it political? If neither, then what?

One night when he and Lady Deborah were having a quiet meal with Commodore Gardner, he broached the subject. He had waited until the ladies had excused themselves. As the two men lit up their pipes and enjoyed a snifter of brandy, Anthony casually asked, "Ever hear of any ransom demands?"

"Why no, I haven't," answered Gardner. "And there's plenty been taken who could and would have paid a handsome sum for their freedom."

Anthony nodded, "That's what I've been thinking. So, do you think someone is giving the pirates 'head money' to make up for lost ransom? If head money is being given, it would take deep pockets."

"Aye," Gardner replied. "Such as a national treasury."

That night as Lady Deborah drew Anthony to her, she stated, "I heard part of your conversation with Commodore Gardner."

"I'm sorry," he replied. "I didn't want you to be troubled with such."

"Oh, I won't be, my love," she answered. "It just makes me more thankful you came along when you did."

"Hmm," said Anthony, a smile breaking out on his face. "Just how thankful?"

"I'll show you," she replied, letting her shawl drop. "Shut the door."

Chapter Twelve

ANTHONY HAD FINALLY GOTTEN a replacement lieutenant for Witzenfeld. Although Gabe and Markham had been commissioned, Anthony was still short of watch-standing officers since his lieutenants had been spread throughout his growing flotilla. He had also acquired two more midshipmen. One was a twelve-year-old pimple faced youth who was as round as he was tall. The lad's name was Joshua Young, and he'd been taken as a favor to Commodore Gardner.

"The young man is a mama's boy and his father wants to wean him from the teat," confided the commodore when he'd approached Anthony about a possible berth. The boy's father was a self-made, well-to-do merchant and he wanted the boy to amount to something besides a spoiled brat. An eventual commission would also make him a gentleman and not just a tradesman's son.

The other youth was Nathan Lavery. He'd been a midshipman for six years and would now be the senior mid. Anthony was concerned about how he'd get along with Davy, but the two hit it off fine. The older boy would be a good influence for Davy.

They'd have to wait and see how young Mr. Young would turn out. His first day on board he cried and whimpered so, that the master had him "kiss the gunner's daughter" for his sniveling. The weaning had begun! After a half dozen by the bosun he "dried it up quick enough." Because Mr. Young was the junior mid, Davy strutted his seniority like a peacock until Buck told him he could find himself at the masthead with his tail feathers plucked. Davy quickly became his old self after the first lieutenant's warning.

Anthony also received confirmation on his broad pennant. However as good as that was, the new lieutenant made Anthony feel that the stars were truly shining down on him. He was heaven sent as far as Anthony was concerned. The man's name was Julian Pope. His father was a former Governor of Barbados and then retired on the island. Since retiring, he'd become a wealthy planter who owned a goodly portion of Barbados and St. John. Pope had entered the Navy as a midshipman under Admiral Rodney in 1760. He had been first lieutenant on the ninety-eight gun, first rate *HMS London* and he'd seen action towards the end of the Seven Year War with France in 1762 and 1763. He'd steadily moved up until he'd made first lieutenant. However, he'd grown tired of cold, dreary English winters, and his father's health was failing. Therefore, he'd applied for any available berth in the West Indies. Pope had been frank with Anthony during their initial meeting. He confided that should his father's health worsen he would resign his commission and take over the family business. Anthony found himself praying for Pope's father to have continued health. Pope had grown up in the West Indies and knew the islands, cays, and inlets like the back of his hand.

With the weather moderating, it was time for the patrols to resume in earnest. Anthony returned to his earlier tactics. He took his flotilla out as a group and deployed them so no ship would ever be out of sight of another. This tactic would allow them to cover a greater area. Anthony also decided to concentrate more towards the Leeward Islands on this patrol. Only St. Martin and Guadeloupe were considered French-held islands, but that was too obvious. If there were a hidden French influence to the ongoing piracy, Anthony didn't think that the rogues would make a French island their base of operation. More likely, a small cay or inlet on a sparsely populated island would serve as a rendezvous. Such a place would offer some shelter from a storm, and yet wouldn't be visible to the casual passerby. A covert cay would be a place they could camp and divide their plunder. Numerous such places were delineated on the local charts the master had acquired, and probably just as many more that had yet to be mapped.

Maybe they would get a break soon. Otherwise, he would be hauling down his new pennant and sailing back to England as a failure. The Leeward Islands seemed to be the area hardest hit recently. If one wanted to catch a pirate, Anthony thought, go to where the pickings are the ripest. Unlike some commanders, Anthony had never been shy of seeking advice from someone with experience. Therefore he sent for Pope, and together with Buck and the master, they went over the few reports they had on the recent raids, plotting the positions on the charts.

Anthony listened closely to Pope's counsel, and was subsequently rewarded by his flotilla's capturing of several small prizes to sail back to English Harbour. They had also burned several "coasters," and had just captured a gun ketch that was definitely French built — the *Shark*.

***

ANTHONY KNEW GABE WANTED the ketch by the time he and Earl had "fetched her up." When Anthony went on board the vessel, he'd heard Gabe declare, "Damme but she's a fine vessel, even after those bastards have abused her so." Being French built, she was not as wide of beam as a British ketch, and slightly longer. Her lines were more sheer and curving with ornate bulwarks and two raked masts. Her transom was beautifully carved, and she carried five six-pounders on each side with a long nine in the fo'c'sle. There also were four swivel guns on the main deck and one at the masthead. These were obviously rigged by the pirates who had taken her. The swivels were good for cutting down opposing crews without causing too much damage to the ship itself. Gabe's only complaint with the vessel was its smell.

After a careful inspection of the ketch, a number of letters were found. They were addressed to various people in England, some to the inhabitants of the local islands, and one to Virginia in the Colonies. Why the letters had not been discarded was a puzzle. The only reason Anthony and his fellow officers could surmise was that some of the letters might contain sailing dates, and maybe a hint at what cargo a ship might be carrying. The letters were also evidence that many ships had fallen prey to the cutthroats.

Upon searching the ketch's storerooms, it was found she carried several barrels of spirits. When Anthony made his way to where the barrels were being "inspected," he found the master had already broached a cask of wine, which he proclaimed far superior to *Drakkar's* wardroom stores. Upon such a proclamation, Anthony had no choice but to order the bung replaced and have it made "ship's stores". He also eyed Silas, who knowing his master, nodded his acknowledgment. Thus a cask was sure to become a part of the commodore's supplies. Several barrels of Jamaican rum were also found. Anthony ordered a barrel to each ship, and the rest poured into the scuppers. Bart was seen shaking his head, muttering what a sad day it was.

The bosun voiced his agreement. "It would've been a man-size job, sir. But I reck'n with Bart, Dagan, and a couple of me mates to 'elp, we could've disposed of it proper like. No use in supplying ole King Neptune, me thinks."

***

ANTHONY NOW HAD NEARLY a hundred pirates as prisoners scattered throughout his flotilla. He had also sent many of his crew back on prizes they had taken. Considering this, he decided it was time to return to English Harbour. He had given the ketch, *Shark*, to Gabe, but warned him it was as prizemaster only for now.

Once he'd got back on *Drakkar*, the master warned, "I just looked at the barometer and I believe we're in for a squall."

Anthony ordered Buck to make ready for the approaching bad weather. Anthony never questioned Peckham on such subjects. Truth be known, he had an achy feeling as well, and felt they may be in for a blow. Without being told, Buck signaled the other ships to prepare for bad weather.

"I don't mean to tell them their jobs, but they don't know it all yet," Buck said by way of explaining the signals. Anthony, without realizing, had turned over more and more of the ship handling to Buck. "*He needs the experience for when he makes post,*" Anthony told himself.

Taking a look around, Anthony could see *Shark*

off to starboard. *Rascal* was further astern but in sight, and was to starboard as well. *LeFoxxe* and *LeCroix* were forward and larboard. The squall hit suddenly and viciously as the master predicted. For several minutes the wind had such force that Anthony was concerned about the ship being taken aback by the wind. During this time he could hear the wind whipping through the rigging. The wind then veered and the sails made a loud flapping sound. Then everything was calm. It was hard to imagine the squall had come and gone in under a half an hour. The watch on deck was soaking wet where they'd been pelted by the rain. Looking aloft for any damage, Anthony sensed the master as he sidled up to him.

"She be intact," Peckham said.

At that time, the lookout that had rode out the squall at his station called down, "Deck there. Signal from *Shark*. Large ship attacking *Rascal*." Anthony whirled toward the master and Buck. Peckham volunteered, "The wind has veered with the squall taking any sound with it."

Buck looked questioningly at Anthony, "Wear ship and beat to quarters?"

"Aye," Anthony replied, a sense of urgency in his voice, "But it'll be over before we get there. Signal *Shark* to keep lookout, but not too close with the enemy. Then signal *LeFoxxe* and *LeCroix* to take station on *Drakkar*. No use sacrificing them."

The experience and training of the crew now

showed. *Drakkar* had come quickly about, and under full sail was beating down on *Rascal*. They were already reaching on *Shark*.

Now that *Rascal* was in sight, Anthony could see she was engulfed in smoke. The helpless schooner appeared dead in the water. Even at this distance, the damage was obvious. The attacking ship was big all right, as big as *Drakkar*, or maybe even bigger; and she was painted black. The smoke was drifting and Anthony could see his foe clearly.

"Her sails are even black," Buck said. "Just like what that poor sod we plucked from the ocean told us."

The lookout called down again, "The ship is tacking, sir, and appears to be opening her larboard gun ports."

Buck caught Anthony looking up and volunteered, "She's carrying every scrap of sail we got, sir." Even as he spoke the pirate ship had closed with *Rascal* and was ready to let loose another broadside.

Anthony ordered Buck, "Fire the bow chasers!"

"Sir?" Buck looked surprised, not sure he'd heard right.

"Fire the damned guns!" Anthony snapped.

No sooner had the order been repeated than the long nines let loose. It suddenly dawned on Buck that Anthony was trying to attract attention to *Drakkar*, and away from *Rascal*. The realization caused him to be embarrassed that he hadn't immediately understood Anthony's actions.

Ignoring Drakkar's bow chasers, the black ship let loose a salvo on *Rascal*. The salvo was ragged, but very effective. Every gun appeared to hit its target. *Rascal's* foremast was over the side; the mainmast was leaning and might fall. The bowsprit was intact, but the jib and fore-staysail, along with most of the rigging, were hanging in the water, acting like a sea anchor. Great sections of the bulwark were blasted away. Guns were up-turned, and a large section of the transom was destroyed.

Anthony had the gun crews continue firing the bow chasers. It was more to vent frustration than for any chance of hitting anything. By the time *Drakkar* was up on *Rascal*, the black ship had run with the wind. Anthony was torn between giving chase and stopping to help *Rascal*. Anthony decided to heave to as the black ship had hauled her wind in the direction of the squall. The likelihood of overtaking the pirate vessel was remote. Once she caught up with the squall, she could easily lose herself. Anthony's decision to not give chase was also based on the fact that his crew had been largely depleted to man the prizes that had already been captured. To defend *Rascal* was one thing. However, to seek out and engage a fully manned pirate vessel the size of the black ship would be not only foolish, but also suicidal, considering the large number of captured pirates already on board *Drakkar*. He'd get no thanks from the Admiralty for having *Drakkar* taken by a bunch of damn cutthroats.

***

BOARDING *RASCAL*, ANTHONY COULD see the destruction and the horror the crew had faced from such an overwhelming foe. Men were lying on deck crushed by upturned guns and fallen spars. Some were groaning in agony, their bodies impaled with large splinters. Others were mercifully dead, so great were their wounds.

"Bloody sodomites," Peckham had shouted, his blood boiling for a fight. "Poxxed bastard won't stand and fight man to man. He has to go after a puppy." The master's sentiment was felt throughout.

The *Rascal* had been battered all right. *Drakkar's* crew members continued to search through the wreckage for survivors among the dead. They lay scattered beneath the fragments of cordage, netting, broken timbers and general carnage.

A couple of petty officers had gathered some of the survivors in an area where the master's cabin had been. Now all that remained of the raised area was a handful of splintered planks. Walking toward this area, Anthony noticed how a layer of smoke seemed to hang in the air a few inches above the deck. This, mixed with the haze left from the recent squall, gave *Rascal's* deck an even more ghastly appearance. Reaching the area where the master's cabin had been, Anthony found Pitts. He'd been laid out on a plank by one of the crew, who was trying to comfort the lieutenant until the surgeon arrived. Pitts had been shot in the chest, and a large splinter protruded from his groin. The surgeon arrived and did a quick exam. He looked at Anthony and shook his head. Pitts tried to sit up, but pain shot through him. Crying out, he fell back on the plank. One of the petty officers had taken a discarded coat and tried to fashion a pillow for him.

"I'm ...I'm sorry, sir," Pitts was speaking, his voice cracked and strained.

"Shh, don't talk now, Merle. Let's get you well," Anthony said taking the lieutenant's hand in his.

"She came right outta the squall, sir, with guns blazing. We never even knew she was there till it was too late. I'm...I'm sorry, sir."

Anthony tried to quiet the dying man and make him comfortable. "It's not your fault, Merle. Rest now."

Silas had brought a small cup of wine and tried to help Pitts take a drink, but the cup was pushed aside.

"I want to ...thank you, sir...for trusting me." Then he was gone.

Anthony had the body taken aboard *Drakkar*. It was a somber group that carried the young lieutenant's body back to the frigate to be made ready for burial. Pitts had been well liked by his fellow officers and the ship's crew, and would be missed. As a flag was being draped over Pitts' body, Anthony gazed upon the crew. Heads were bowed in respect for Pitts and other crew members who had been slain by *Reaper's* attack. Tears drained from eyes and dripped onto the deck. Anthony gave a nod to Buck who ordered "hats off." When there was silence, Anthony read the customary passage from the Bible and Book of Common Prayer. After reading the passage, "Unto Almighty God we commend the soul of our brother departed, and we commit his body to the deep," the plank was lifted and Pitts' body sank into the Caribbean waters along with the other fallen crew members.

After a respectful pause, Dawkins spoke what they all felt, "Bloody sodomites has hit us'ns good. They got our 'tention but they's gonna pay. I lost some good mates along with Mr. Pitts and I don't take kindly how the bastards went about it. We's with you, Cap'n."

"Aye, aye," other crew members chorused.

"It's hard to find a silver lining after what we've gone through today, Captain," Lieutenant Dunn stated, "But if there is one, the damned pirates has embittered the men so that I wouldn't want to try to stop them from butchering the rogues."

"Aye," Buck joined in, "I doubt they'd take kindly to taking prisoners."

Anthony had to agree. A new air of determination seemed to prevail. However, burying those whom you put in harm's way was one of the most difficult parts of command. Anthony couldn't help but feel a sense of guilt, but he knew he must carry on. He had to carry on.

***

LATER, BUCK, THE CARPENTER, and the bosun met with Anthony. "Most of the damage was done 'betwixt wind and water'," the carpenter reported. "Therefore, Rascal will float. However, with the foremast gone and the mainmast hit, it will take awhile to get her re-rigged and back to English Harbour. I'll want to fish the mainmast, proper like, otherwise I'm not sure she'll take the strain."

Buck spoke up, "Sir, let's put some of the prisoners to work putting *Rascal* back together. Lieutenant Dunn's marines can keep them covered."

"Aye," chimed in the bosun. "And a bare-o-net in the arse once in awhile to keep the whoresons moving wouldn't be amiss, I'm thinking."

Bart had walked up during the last of the conversation and heard the bosun's comments. He'd come to tell Anthony that Gabe and Dagan were alongside, and would be present any minute. Seeing the look in Anthony's eyes almost frightened him. He'd never seen such a determined look. He spoke his feelings aloud, "I wouldn't want to be that damn pirate as he headed back toward *Drakkar*. 'The Grim Reaper.' Well, he ain't seen bloody grim like the shat for brains the sod is gona see now he's done crossed with me Cap'n."

Buck wondered if Bart would ever stop calling

Anthony captain, but he agreed with Bart's statement.

Dagan had overtaken Bart, and overhearing his words, added, "Aye! I feels his time is nigh but 'e won't go quietly. He'll be gone, but not quietly."

Chapter Thirteen

THE SIGHT OF THE small flotilla limping into English Harbour created a different type of stir than previous times when Anthony's squadron proudly sailed its prizes in. Much of *Rascal's* damage had been temporarily repaired, but huge scars still remained, attesting to the battering that she'd taken. Commodore Gardner had been rowed out to meet them in a guard boat.

Upon hearing how *Reaper* had viciously attacked *Rascal*, the commodore waxed livid. "He's trying to goad you, make you make a mistake, Gil, so be careful. You're hurting him with all the prizes you've taken and men you've either killed or captured. He's got to do something."

Anthony understood the wisdom in Gardner's words. Before going ashore, the commodore vowed, "We'll fix up *Rascal*. The dockyard will work night and day if they have to, but we'll have repairs completed so *Rascal* can return to her duties before you know it."

The entire attitude seemed to change on the island of Antigua. The islanders had come to look at the men under Anthony's command as their own. Now, everyone felt the loss of Lieutenant Pitts and many of his crew. The increasing reports of hostilities between England and the Colonies only added to the people's anger. The hostilities were now rumored to have gone beyond verbal. The master of a mail packet had just returned from Halifax. Word had gotten to the commander in chief of that station that colonial men in whale boats would dash out of hidden creeks and coves to harass British ships riding at anchor in Boston Harbour. The master went on to say they had removed channel buoys and had gone so far as to burn lighthouses. Needless to say, the concern was great, and British forces in the colonies were having a time deciding who was loyal and who was not. It was not uncommon for a father to profess loyalty to the crown while his son openly chose rebellion. Some of the would-be loyalists kept quiet for fear of reprisals from rebellious colonists. The British soldiers stationed in the colonies were vastly out-numbered, and could do little by way of affording protection. Many felt Lord North could have done more to halt the escalating difficulties.

Standing behind the desk in his office, Commodore Gardner peered down at the ships anchored in the harbour. He had to squint to keep the sun from hurting his eyes. Angrily, he snatched the curtains together to block out the blinding rays.

"Lord North underestimates the colonies,

Gil, I tell you. He takes them too lightly. They'll fight and fight like no enemy we've dealt with in the past. I doubt they'll stand at ranks and fire as if on parade. Nay, it'll be hit and run. They've fought the native Indians, and they've learned their tactics well."

Peering once more out of his office window, Commodore Gardner made one more comment. It was more a prediction. "Lord North and Parliament has bitten off more than they can chew. If he doesn't learn to respect the abilities of the colonials, we'll lose this war. Mark my word sir, we'll lose."

***

AFTER LEAVING GOVERNMENT HOUSE, Anthony went to "the cottage." Lady Deborah was waiting and offered a warm greeting. However, she could see Anthony was despondent and angry over the news from the colonies, on top of *Rascal's* near destruction by the *Reaper*. But beyond Anthony's anger was a feeling of despair and hurt from losing Merle Pitts and so many of *Rascal's* crew. Deborah had never seen this side of her man, and was moved by his sincerity. *"He cares for those he commands. No wonder his officers and men respond to him as they do,"* she thought.

"He tried so hard to please me," Anthony was saying, speaking of Pitts. "He was always eager and carefree unless the need arose. Then he could be very serious. He would have made a fine captain." Anthony had written to Pitts's father. The letter included not only comments about the young man's bravery and ultimate sacrifice, but also some of the pleasurable times they'd had. He also included a lock of Pitts's hair. When Anthony had finished the letter he laid it down and said, "Words seem so hollow. How do you tell a father his son is gone, and at the same time try to ease his pain by telling him Merle died heroically while doing his duty in some far corner of the world that he's probably never even heard of? That his body was buried at sea and therefore there will be no grave to visit? How do you say all these things? It sounds so cheap saying he gave his life for England."

Anthony took his pipe and walked to the porch to light up. Seeing the letter lying open on the table, Deborah picked it up and read it. Reading the letter she couldn't help but cry. Laying the letter on the table and using her handkerchief to wipe the tears from her eyes, she rushed out onto the porch and took Anthony in her arms.

"Oh, Gil, you wonderful man. Your letter was so perfect. I wanted to stand up and shout. No one could have said better about Merle and made him sound so heroic. His father will be hurt, but he'll be proud."

Later that night as Anthony was holding Deborah, she snuggled even closer and whispered to him, "Ever consider marrying an old widow woman who has proved she's utterly shameless?"

Anthony sat up, wide-awake. He looked her in

the eyes and said, "Do you really mean it?"

"Yes, my brave captain."

Anthony pulled her closer and kissed her. Their lovemaking seemed to make him feel whole again. Later in the wee hours of the morning he spoke, "Deborah!"

"Yes, Gil."

"You've made me the happiest man in the world."

"And I'm the happiest woman in the world," she replied.

"You hungry?" Anthony asked.

"No."

"I'm not talking about food, Deborah."

"Oh, you dirty man. I'm starved."

***

THE WEDDING WAS PLANNED for May.

"I'd like to be a June bride, but that is too long. So May it'll be," Deborah had commented. It would take that long to get announcements and letters to the respective families.

Anthony was torn about what to do in regards to his invitations. He didn't want to offend Gabe or his mother by not extending an invitation. However, Maria would not want to be embarrassed by being present if Anthony's mother were there. Knowing his mother, Anthony was sure she'd say something to insult Maria for being his father's mistress. Another thought came to mind. Did Mother even know about Gabe? Anthony didn't think so but wasn't sure. How would he handle that situation? He intended to ask Gabe to be his best man and if mother came how did he introduce the two? "Mother, this is one of my lieutenants." No, he'd not dishonor Gabe or his father in such a manner. One look and mother would know the truth. *Father could never deny Gabe*, Anthony thought. *Well, I'll warn Gabe and we'll cross that bridge when we have to. However, in regards to Maria, what should I do?*

I'll leave it up to Becky, Anthony decided finally. Mother has been "ill" lately and it was possible she wouldn't be able to make the voyage. If she wasn't able to travel, Becky would extend an invitation to Maria, encouraging her to make the voyage with Becky's family.

***

DEBORAH AND ANTHONY INVITED Gabe, Bart, and Dagan to dine with them the following evening. They wanted them to be the first to know of their plans. Deborah was apprehensive, but Anthony hushed her fears by kissing her lips.

"They all love you and will be happy for us," Anthony said. "Just wait and see."

Dinner had been served, and the men poked fun over Anthony's getting fat on such fare. After a full meal and a succulent pudding for dessert, the men gathered on the porch to enjoy their pipes. One of the servants brought out a decanter of claret and fresh glasses. As the glasses were filled, Deborah walked out on the porch as if on cue. When the men stood up, Anthony looked at them...his friends...his family.

He cleared his throat and said, "Men, this is a special occasion for which you all were invited. I look on each of you as a very special part of my life. Some would say family. We in the Navy know it goes beyond family. Ties that bind us by both blood and battle have formed a union no landsman could fully understand. I have asked for another union, and Lady Deborah has graciously accepted my humble proposal. I...we...have invited you three here tonight to share in our joy before it is publicly announced." Anthony looked at the men who stood before him, their mouths agape. Concerned about their acceptance, he continued, "It's been no secret how I feel about Lady Deborah." Before Anthony could finish, the men's shouts and cries of congratulations interrupted him.

"We's been wondering when you'd get enough wind in ye sails to ask," Bart stated in his strong accent. All it took was those few seconds for Anthony's words to sink in before they reacted, as he knew the men would.

Anthony pulled Lady Deborah near, enjoying the good-natured bantering to which the three men were subjecting their commanding officer.

"I knew you was smitten, Cap'n. Told Mr. Buck I did, I jes' know'd it," Bart continued.

Gabe turned to Lady Deborah and japed, "Are you sure, Madam? You don't know him the same as we do."

Dagan surprised everyone. He used the end of his pipe to tap on his wineglass and get everyone's attention. "Gentlemen," he said, "A toast! To the commodore and his beautiful lady. May you always have fair winds and following seas."

"Hear, hear," they all said in unison as they drained their glasses.

Anthony was taken aback by Dagan's manner, and his elegance. This was another side of this mysterious man he'd neither seen nor imagined.

Anthony then placed his hand on Gabe's shoulders, surprising him. "Gabe, would you do me the honor of being my best man?"

That Gabe was moved was obvious to all present. "Of course," he muttered. "But what about Mr. Buck?"

Anthony looked directly into Gabe's eyes as he responded. "Rupert is my first lieutenant and a dear friend. But you, Gabe, are my brother." Then they all hugged, and Anthony suffered through Bart's telling and re-telling of the incident where he'd had the cocked pistol in his pants pointed at his "wedding tackle."

Later, after retiring for the evening, Anthony asked Deborah, "If the gun had gone off and I was ah... ere... crippled, would you still have agreed to marry me?"

"Huh," was all she said.

A few days later, after the engagement had been made public, the bosun questioned, "Where you headed this time, Bart?"

"To help Lady Deborah pick out a wedding gift for the cap'n, if it's anything to ye."

The bosun snorted, "The commodore, you idget. Yew's the cox'n and still calls him cap'n."

"That's cause he's still me cap'n...me and the lady's cap'n, that is."

"You and the lady's? Yewed think ye was bloody family."

"Oh, I is," quipped Bart. "Jus' ask the cap'n if ye don't believes me. He'll tell ye!"

Chapter FOURTEEN

THE MAIL PACKET, *HERON,* had just set sail. Anthony watched and couldn't help but feel a degree of envy for her commander. He was only a lieutenant, but when he stepped aboard his ship he was given the same honor as a captain on a first rate. It was the freedom that Anthony envied. The *Heron's* skipper was free of the humdrum duties associated with the fleet. Governors and senior naval officers, such as Commodore Gardner, who was starved for the latest news and gossip, generally welcomed him as an honored guest.

It was rumored that a senior admiral had held up sailing orders for an entire fleet until a mail packet commander could finish a particular juicy tale about a Member of Parliament coming home and almost catching his wife having sex with a young frigate captain. The lady in question heard her husband, who was much older, come puffing in the house and start up the stairs to their bedroom. The lady jumped out of bed and quickly put on a very revealing gown that left nothing to the imagination. She then stood in the doorway blocking her husband's view of the room. During this time, the frigate captain hastily gathered up his clothes that thankfully were piled next to the bed. Scooping everything together he slid under the bed. As quietly as he could, he began to dress, paying particular care so he wouldn't make any noise and thus be discovered. The lady made a valiant attempt to entice her husband to partake of her favors. After some coaxing, she was able to arouse the man to activity. The captain had to lie under the bed, which groaned under the weight of the lady and her husband. A great sag in the mattress gave the captain cause for concern, and he had to work his way to one side of the bed to keep from being pinned down between the bed and the floor. After a while the sounds from the two having sex and the constant groan and squeak of the bed lulled the captain's senses and he dozed off. He was not sure how long he'd slept when a sudden loud sound awakened him. At first he wasn't sure if it had been a loud snore or if one of the two above had expelled a resounding bout of flatulence. However, a certain foul odor started to permeate the air. The smell had been bad enough with the husband's shoes not a foot away from the captain's face. Now this new odor, combined with the shoes, was overwhelming. The captain, who had always suffered from a weak stomach, found himself gagging and couldn't crawl from beneath the bed quick enough, spewing his gastric contents from the side of the bed, through the door, and down the stairs. As the captain made his urgent departure, he woke up his lady friend who immediately set about cleaning up the mess. Her husband slept through the entire process. The lady thought she'd removed all signs of her lover having been present and therefore went back to bed.

"Did the old man ever become the wiser?" the admiral asked the lieutenant.

"Aye, sir. In the morning when he put on his shoes."

***

MAIL CALL HAD BEEN passed, and men were gathering in little groups before the mail packet was out of sight. Anthony and Deborah's engagement and wedding announcements were on the packet. Anthony saw the surgeon sitting on a crate near the forecastle with several men gathered around him. One was very near him and the others sat a respectful distance away. The surgeon was reading mail for the men who couldn't read. Anthony was never certain if the surgeon was being kind-hearted or if he was just nosy.

Bart strode up and declared, "Funny ain't it, Cap'n. Half them buggers can't read or write, but they's always getting mail."

It did amaze Anthony. He knew several officers that not only read letters for the men but also would even write home for them upon occasions. Sometimes a seaman who was more educated would provide these services for his mates.

Anthony had gone back to his cabin and had just finished a letter from his agent in London when the marine sentry hit the deck with the butt of his musket and shouted, "Lieutenant Anthony, Zur." The loud noise and the marine's shout startled Anthony. Without thinking he cursed, "Damme man, but we're between decks, not on the parade field."

As Gabe entered, Anthony was still muttering, "Thinks he'll make corporal, but he's lucky I don't keel haul him." Gabe had to laugh at his brother, causing Anthony to smile at his irritability.

"Sit down Gabe. Silas, a glass if you will. Claret would not be amiss." Anthony bellowed to his servant, mocking the sentry's recent outburst.

Gabe had become a more frequent visitor since he'd been asked to be "best man." He always made sure it was at appropriate times, such as when "make and mend" had been passed. Today, Gabe had a letter in his hand, which he handed to Anthony, and said, "Does this mean what I think it does?"

After peering at the letter, Anthony responded. "If you're asking if you're a wealthy man, then the answer is yes."

Anthony had talked Gabe into letting his prize agent in London handle Gabe's prize and head money. Anthony tapped his own letter which he'd laid on the table and said, "It appears we're both well off. There's enough to hold us for a while if we wind up on half pay after this commission is complete."

Gabe looked at his brother, suddenly very serious. "Do you think we'll wind up on the beach, sir?"

Anthony found that even he was disturbed by that question. Not about the possibility of being without a ship, but the very likelihood of war with the colonies. "No, Gabe. With the shaping hostilities, I believe as the commodore does. Lord North has pushed too far, and we...men like you and me...will pay for his arrogance. Soldiers and sailors alike will die. I only pray we are spared."

"Dagan has family in the colonies."

The statement was so out of the blue Anthony was taken aback. "Dagan does?"

"Yes, sir. He and mother's family lived in Guernsey. They were Huguenots and moved to Guernsey from France thinking they'd find greater acceptance being French Protestants. But life was hard. Dagan's father, my grandfather, was first mate on a snow and eventually was given his own ship, but had to move to Chatham. Without family being close by, Dagan's uncle moved to the colonies with Lord Burgoyne. Lord Burgoyne's offer of land and horses were more than he could resist. Now Uncle Andre has a large farm and breeds some of the finest horses in Virginia."

After Gabe left, Anthony found himself dwelling on just how little he knew of Gabe's family on his mother's side. He'd believed the rumors of Gabe's mother being a gypsy lady because it had been convenient. Dagan certainly had the appearance and mystique of a gypsy. But just what did being a gypsy mean anyway? The thought was still with Anthony when he drifted off to sleep that evening. He awoke sweating. He had been dreaming that Dagan had charmed and then beheaded a great sea monster that was about to engulf *Drakkar* and her entire crew. In his dream, Dagan had been a sorcerer. A gypsy sorcerer.

Chapter Fifteen

GABE WAS HELPING WITH some re-fittings on board *Rascal*. While making sure the repairs were being done satisfactorily, Gabe and Lieutenant Pope had been in a general discussion of possible ways to locate the pirate's lair. Gabe noticed a shadow on the deck, and when he looked up he found Bart and Anthony peering down at their handiwork.

"Told ye," Bart was saying to Anthony. "'E'll make a fair bosun's mate if he ain't found suited to be an officer."

"Damn you, Bart," Gabe snorted.

"See 'e's already talking like a bosun, Cap'n. Bless me if 'e ain't."

Having given the two time to insult one another good-naturedly, Anthony said to Gabe, "Lieutenant Buck says you got some ideas on how to go about finding the pirate's supply base."

"Yes sir," Gabe started, "I've been discussing this with Lieutenant Pope, and it's really his idea. He thinks we might use *Shark* to get a closer look at several of the coves and inlets around some of the smaller islands and cays where we're likely to find the pirates. There is liable to be places the other ships can't get close to without causing a stir."

"You think they'll just let you sail in, spy on their operation, and then allow you to sail off again without cutting at least a few throats?"

"No sir. We thought we might get the loan of some marines from Lieutenant Dunn to give us a few extra fighting men. We'd keep them out of sight of course, and leave off our uniforms, dressing like some of the rogues we've captured. We will rendezvous at certain times and locations."

"What if you get into trouble?" Anthony asked his energetic brother.

"Well sir, you'll always be close — stay in sight of the masthead lookout. If there's trouble we can send up a flare."

Anthony nodded. He'd been thinking along those same lines. Anthony also knew Gabe wanted command of the ketch, but this was a job for someone who had more experience. He would let Gabe go along as second, but Lieutenant Pope, who in the past had commanded a cutter and a brig, had the necessary experience as well as the knowledge of the local waters. Looking at Gabe, Anthony said, "Who do you think should lead this search?"

"Er...I would like to sir, but I'd be glad to second Lieutenant Pope. I'm sure he'll be your choice."

"Aye, that he is," Anthony agreed. "But don't

you worry. You'll get your command soon enough. And who knows? This little trip may even present us with another little prize to fatten your purse."

This comment brought a smile to Gabe's face even though Anthony sensed his disappointment.

***

IT HAD BEEN THREE days since the flotilla had beat its way out of English Harbour on a heading that most merchantmen would use going to Barbados. *Drakkar* and her consorts would lie hove to or move along under reduced sail while the ketch, *Shark*, made her way through the shallows around Dominica, Martinique, St. Lucia and finally St. Vincent. Now it was time to rendezvous as planned and sail into Barbados. Though disappointed at coming up empty-handed in their pursuit of the pirate's lair, Anthony had to admit Pope knew his business. The trip was not a total waste, as Anthony felt the experience was needed for the new hands. They were already decent seamen, but they needed to learn the Navy way of doing things.

As McMorgan, the bosun, was so fond of saying, "They's the right way, the wrong way, and then there's the King's way. From this day forward, lads, it's me duty to teach you the King's way."

Standing on his quarterdeck, Anthony watched ships of various sizes and descriptions coming and going, as *Drakkar* made her approach into Barbados. Most were traders, but a few were naval vessels and one was a sleek yacht. Small boats could be seen plying their way between shore and anchored ships. A water hoy was tied up along side a brig. Lord Howe was there in his flagship, the sixty-four gun *Eagle*. She was old, her keel having been laid somewhere around 1740. She had been with Rodney's squadron off Cape Finisterre in 1747. *Drakkar,* having begun her life as a sixty-four, suggested comparison to *Eagle. Drakkar's* lines appeared to be sleeker, and she didn't appear to be as broad in the beam. *Eagle* would never have been the fast sailor that *Drakkar* is, Anthony decided.

"Damn the French. But they knew how to build ships," Anthony said aloud without realizing it.

"Sir?"

Anthony looked down. Lavery, one of the new mids, looked puzzled. "I'm sorry sir, you were saying?"

Feeling embarrassed for speaking his thoughts aloud Anthony said, "It's time we honor the flag, is it not? Prepare to fire our salute."

"Aye, sir," Lavery answered. He then sped away to relay the message to the gunner who was already prepared to render honors.

Bart was laying out Anthony's best coat when he walked into his quarters. "Silas will help you change sir, while I see to it that the gig's ready," Bart said and then departed. He had been around long enough to know the Admiral would likely signal "repair on board" as soon as the last shot was fired and the salute had been rendered.

***

Lord Howe cheerfully greeted Anthony and offered refreshment while congratulating him on hoisting his pennant. Anthony quickly filled the admiral in on their success and failures to this point.

"My word, but the man sounds like a black-hearted devil," Lord Howe had said upon hearing how *Reaper* and her cohorts were slaughtering their captives.

"Means to anger you so you'll make a mistake," the admiral exclaimed. "Keep your wits about you. Otherwise..."

Anthony had noticed Lord Howe kept watching his door as if expecting someone to enter. Finally the flag lieutenant did so.

"Excuse me, sir. It is time, my Lord."

"I beg your forgiveness, Gil," Lord Howe said. "I have a meeting with the Governor. We've just been told things are heating up in the Colonies, and I'm going to have to try to deal with it. Bad business, Gil. Bad business."

Anthony stood and shook Lord Howe's hand. Almost as an afterthought Lord Howe called, "Flags. Have you not been introduced to the commodore? His father and I were friends." Turning back to Anthony, Lord Howe offered his condolences. "I'm sorry to hear he's gone, Gil."

Returning his attention to the flag lieutenant, Howe said, "Our commodore's father was known as 'Fighting James Anthony'. Like his father, our guest has already made a name for himself as a fighter. I expect he'll follow in his father's footsteps and raise his own flag before long."

***

AFTER RETURNING TO *DRAKKAR* and finishing a light evening meal of kidney pie, wine and a small dish of plum duff, Anthony was reading his log and going over his entries when the marine sentry announced, "Lt. Anthony, zur." Gabe entered, trying hard to appear normal, but he was obviously the worse for drink.

"I say, Gabe. Are you in your cups, sir?"

Anthony was somewhat taken aback by Gabe's appearance. Nodding his head in the affirmative, Gabe managed an, "Aye, sir," with the "sir" being belched. "Sorry, sir, but my present state is the result of upholding the honor of the Navy, sir. More precisely, the honor of *Drakkar*."

"Hmm! How so?" Anthony questioned.

"Well sir, Julian, ere Mr. Pope, Stephen Earl, and myself stopped in at a tavern for a wet. We were enjoying our first tankard, when this bullock major comes in and tells Nancy she ..."

Anthony had held up his hand stopping Gabe in mid sentence, "Nancy? Who's Nancy?"

"Oh, she's a sassy little wench who was trying to decide which of the three of us would offer her the most pleasure when we bedded her."

Anthony's eyes widened. "You were all going to bed the same wench?" he asked, not sure if he wanted to hear more.

"Oh no, sir," Gabe assured him. "Just the one she chose. That's when this bloody bullock said if she truly wanted pleasure, she needed to forget about us Navy slobs and cast her lot with him — a marine, a true man."

"I see," said Anthony, who was now starting to warm to what promised to be a good story.

After pausing to collect his thoughts and steady himself, Gabe continued. "Then Caleb..."

Once again Anthony interrupted, "Is Caleb the bullock major?"

Gabe was shaking his head. "No sir. He's a doctor from the Colonies who got run out of Massachusetts after being caught 'flagrante delicto' with the governor's niece."

"My God!" Anthony exclaimed, not believing his ears.

This time Gabe was shaking his head negatively but responded in the affirmative, "Caleb said a finer piece of mutton didn't exist."

Now Anthony was shaking his head. "Pray tell me how this doctor is involved in upholding *Drakkar's* honor?"

"Oh, yes sir. It was Caleb-that's the ...belch doc...tor, who said we should have a competition, and the victor would enjoy the wench's pleasure."

This is getting interesting, Anthony thought. As Gabe seemed to have lost his train of thought,

Anthony said, "Please continue."

"Er…, we decided to have a drinking contest. The major brought in two of his bullock mates, and we, Stephen, Julian and I, took them on. I won! I was the last man standing."

Unable to hide his amusement, Anthony asked, "Was the lass worth it?"

"Oh, ah, well sir, the contest took so long Nancy got tired of waiting and went upstairs and bedded Caleb."

"Well, damme," burst out Anthony, laughing. "I hope the good doctor don't get the pox."

"Oh no sir, he won't," Gabe replied all at once very seriously. "Caleb had a new condrum."

"That was a good story. It sounds like you've had an eventful evening Gabe. Is that why you wanted to see me?"

"Oh no sir," said Gabe, realizing he hadn't broached the subject that was the reason for his visit. "I just about forgot, sir," Gabe said, now trying very hard to not weave on his feet as a gentle swell caused *Drakkar* to rise then settle, "The doctor wanted to know if he might take passage back to English Harbour with us. He has relations there he's going to visit."

Anthony, somewhat surprised Gabe would make such a request, stated, "I'm sure he'd be more comfortable if he obtained passage with some merchant vessel or coastal trader."

"He can't, sir."

"He can't?" frowned Anthony.

"No sir. He's broke; he doesn't have any money. I had to pay his tavern bill," declared Gabe.

All at once there was a loud shrieking sound, almost like a scream, on the deck overhead. Men could be heard cursing in loud excited voices, the sound of feet as the watch scurried around on deck, and then more shouts.

"What the hell?" Anthony cried as he bounded from his chair, heading topside.

"It sounds like the doctor's ape," Gabe said nonchalantly. Anthony stopped dead in his tracks.

"His ape?"

"Aye, sir. A cute little bugger he is too, but somewhat difficult when he's in his cups."

"The monkey drinks?"

"It's an ape, sir. Not a monkey. He's an ape. But aye, sir, it drinks."

***

THE NEXT MORNING ANTHONY was going over last evening's story and subsequent events with Buck. Buck had been a guest of the first lieutenant from *Eagle*, and therefore had missed the excitement.

"I hope Lord Howe didn't hear the damned commotion. Can you imagine his being awakened and training a glass on *Drakkar* only to see a damned ape being chased through the riggings by the watch?"

Buck couldn't help but laugh, trying to imagine the sight. Anthony snorted, "Laugh if you will, sir. But when I'm sitting on the beach collecting half pay, I'll have company — and that's no error."

Chapter Sixteen

THE AROMA OF ROASTED kid filled the air and Anthony heard his stomach growling. Bart strolled up to him and commented, "It were a nice thing you did for the crew, sir. Roast kid will be like a special feast after months of salt pork."

Anthony had bought six goats for the crew while in Barbados. "Well, Bart, if the damn goat tastes as good as it smells, it'll be well worth the effort and hassle of getting them on board."

"Aye, sir. The smell 'as got me mouth watering and belly rumbling."

It was a different odor that funneled its way up from the galley. Several of the crew were inching closer to the hatch to make their way down to their mess when dinner was called. Anthony and Bart had both noticed how the men were anticipating the evening meal.

Anthony looked at Bart and again said, "I hope it tastes as good as it smells."

Without thinking, Bart replied, "Oh it do sir, it truly does. Silas done fixed up a shoulder and it's prime."

Anthony just shook his head at the cox'n

and said, "And you felt no need to wait. You just helped yourself?"

"Nay sir. I just sorta caught up some of the drippings on a biscuit, as they was going to waste anyway."

While trying to act perturbed, Anthony spotted Caleb's ape. "Tell me, Bart. How do you suppose ape would taste?"

Bart stared at Anthony for a second before the two started laughing at the question. "I don't rightly know, sir, but I believes I'd pass on it given the opportunity. I surely would."

***

"DECK THERE. SIGNAL FROM *Shark*. Sail fine on the starboard quarter."

Turning back to Bart, Anthony said, "I woke up with a feeling this morning that this day would prove to be eventful. Maybe today will be a turning point."

"Mr. Davy," Anthony called to the midshipman. "Aloft with you. Take your glass and remember all you've been taught." Anthony halted the eager boy as he headed up the shrouds. "Don't be afraid to ask the lookout if you are not sure. He's experienced. Learn all you can, and don't be afraid to trust your men."

"Aye, sir. I'll do you proud." Then Davy was on his way up to the masthead. He shunned the lubbers hole by climbing the futtock shrouds like a seasoned sailor. The lookout was smiling down as he moved over to give Davy room.

As Anthony's gaze returned to the deck, he saw Buck standing there grinning at him.

"Does something humor you, Mr. Buck?"

"Nay sir. Just admiring how you handled the youngster."

"Well sir, I'd admire it if you'd demonstrate some of your leadership and get the crew fed and back on deck. Then see if we can clear for action in a dog-watch or less."

Hearing the friendly banter between Anthony and the first lieutenant, the master couldn't contain his laughter. "Ho! Ho! Ho! A dog-watch or less. Ho! Ho! Ho!" Laughing so with his huge belly shaking and his long white hair flowing in the wind, it was hard to picture the jolly old master as a dangerous man. However, more than one had made the mistake of underestimating him by his looks, not realizing the savagery with which he wielded his blade when his fighting blood was up.

***

A SUDDEN SQUALL HAD given temporary relief from the sultry heat. The reprieve had since succumbed to a blazing sun that was making tar bubble from the seams between the deck planks. Gabe had long since given up on finding a cool spot. Enduring the heat, he focused his thoughts on the strange sail that they were overtaking. Pope had just descended the shrouds where he'd gone up for a better look.

"Looks like she may be a slaver, or was."

"She's poorly handled if she's a slaver. They usually fly," Gabe commented.

"My thoughts as well," Pope replied. "Either she's got a lubber for a master, which I doubt, or she wants to be overtaken without being obvious about it."

"Think she can see *Drakkar's* sails?" Gabe asked as he squinted his eyes peering in *Drakkar's* direction.

"I doubt it."

The men aboard "*Shark*" were in civilian dress, with a green armband on the left arm to identify them as friend versus foe if hand to hand fighting erupted. The ketch had to look the same as any other coastal vessel one would expect to find plying its trade in these waters. Therefore, the crew's attire had to look the part. Gabe's thoughts returned to the heat.

"Those marines hiding between decks will likely have their brains roasted to the point they'll be of no use if we don't get them some air soon."

Pope agreed and called to Dagan, "My compliments to the marine sergeant. Tell him to allow two or three of his men up on deck at a time for about fifteen minutes, and then rotate them. We'll soon need them ready with their wits about them, I'm thinking."

It took another turn of the glass for the strange ship to become clearly visible from the *Shark's* deck. "She's been in the trade all right," Pope volunteered. "Can you smell her, Gabe? It's a smell you won't soon forget once you know it."

"We appear to be overtaking her quickly now," Gabe said, noticing he could make out specific details on the ship they were bearing down on.

At the same instant, the lookout called down, "Deck there. She's luffed, sir! Now she's gone about! She's gone about!" he cried again frantically. "She's opening her gunports!"

"Damnation," Pope exclaimed. "Everybody down. Get down on deck now!" he bellowed his order to the crew. No sooner had Pope's orders been shouted than a broadside from the pirate ship tore into *Shark's* rigging and upper deck. Lying flat on the deck, the air above seemed to come alive with the sound of grape, not unlike bees around a hive. Langrage shot was wreaking havoc upon *Shark's* rigging. The intent was to stop but not destroy the ship, yet take as much human life as possible. The broadside might have been ragged, but it had been vicious. Riggings and shrouds were shredded. Torn cordage and severed blocks plummeted to the deck, injuring several hands as it fell upon them. Musket balls thudded into the deck as the pirates fired at the dazed crew as if they were fish in a bowl. Then there was return fire from *Shark*. Dagan had gotten a swivel gun into action, and it had done enough damage to give *Shark's* crew a brief reprieve from the musketry. Pope and Gabe were now on their feet giving orders and organizing the men, getting them into action.

"Grapnels! He's going to grapple," Pope shouted. "Cut the grapnel lines!"

Gabe nodded, then turned and ordered a master's mate. "Send up the flares. I just hope it's not too damn late."

The pirate's guns had damaged timbers, planks, and a good section of the bulwark in addition to the destruction aloft. Thank God for Pope's sudden order to get down or they'd not have enough men left to fight the ship. Musket fire from the pirates had started anew. Shots whined overhead, and the master's mate Gabe had ordered to send up the flare fell kicking, his face reduced to a bloody pulp. *Sharks'* swivel banged again sharply. Its canister cut down a number of the pirates as they had grouped amidships making ready to board. The screaming herd had been reduced to a writhing mass.

"Boarders! Repel boarders!" Pope was shouting. This was the cue for the marines to come on deck. Their sudden appearance gave life to *Shark's* defenders, but still more grapnels were flying through the air to replace those cut or shot away. The marine sharpshooters were doing their best to cut down the enemy as they attempted to board *Shark*, but the numbers were too great.

The distinct sound of the swivel gun filled the air again. "*Damn,*" Gabe thought. "*That had to have been the second shot in under a minute.*"

Dagan was doing his part. The canister from the swivel gun acted like a great scythe, cutting down another group of boarders as they were attempting to come across. Screams, curses, and cries of pain were intertwined with the ring of metal-on-metal as cutlasses clashed, along with the sounds of gunfire as pistols and muskets went off. Gabe felt a glancing blow to his shoulder as a pirate plummeted to the deck, his eyes glaring, but not seeing, as a handspike had been buried in his skull. Almost out of breath, Gabe's arm felt like lead. The constant jar upon jar as he fended off one cutthroat after another had caused his arm to go numb. He felt himself giving ground. There were too many. A musket or pistol ball burned the side of his scalp and blood started to flow. Gabe tried to keep his focus on the man in front of him. The pirate sensed victory with the sudden flow of blood down Gabe's face. Before he could press his advantage, however, a marine shot the man, jamming a musket to his head and pulling the trigger.

Pope's group was all but surrounded as they made their stand beneath the mainmast. Gabe and his band had been backed against the aft rail. They could retreat no further. One more step and they'd be in the sea. "Damn it. Where the hell was *Drakkar*?" Dagan let loose with another round of canister. Its effect was murderous as it cut down a swarm of pirates who were engaging Pope's group.

Bleeding from his wounds, Gabe now seemed to be in a fog, not fully aware of, or in control of his body. He was now acting on instinct alone. He heard the rasp of steel as he warded off another lunge. He was surrounded now. He deflected yet another blow, but felt a sharp, searing pain in his shoulder. Gabe felt himself sliding in blood. Whether it was his or someone else's, he didn't know. A gunshot exploded next to Gabe, and a blood spattered pirate crashed into him. The man was clenched in a death's grip with one of *Shark's* crew, neither willing to give. From somewhere in Gabe's dazed mind, he heard someone shouting, "Strike, will you strike?"

"Strike be damned," he muttered in his last conscious thought.

***

"EASY SIR. EASY NOW. We're all here sir!" Slowly the fog started to clear. *Have I been dreaming*? Gabe wondered. A sob escaped his lips as the pain in his head, his shoulder, and side became very real. His eyes seemed to fog over again, but in the mist he saw his brother and he reached out.

"Gil!"

"Easy lad," muttered the American doctor, Caleb. He was with Anthony. Then Dagan was offering him water. Everything went black after that.

For several days, Gabe went in and out of consciousness. Fever wracked his body, and delirium twisted his senses. He talked to his father, and called out to his mother. He heard voices.

"Gabe, it's Gil. I'm here for you."

In his fog, he saw Dagan come and go. He recalled whispers and hushed voices, and women. He heard women's voices. He recalled trying to rise up only to be pushed back down. "Easy man. Don't rush it. You need your rest." Then it was all black again.

Rain-it sounded like rain outside. Gabe opened his eyes. It was raining outside. He could hear it. But where was he? He didn't hear the familiar sounds associated with a ship. This was not his cot. He felt the covers, all soft and sweet smelling. He felt a slight pain as he moved. His clothes. Where was his clothes? He was naked beneath the frilly covers.

"Well, look who is back from the dead," Caleb said. He had entered the bedroom and witnessed Gabe's return to consciousness. Gabe attempted a smile, but felt a twinge and stiffness along his scalp as he did so.

"Ah lad, it's beat up you are, and somewhat the worse for wear. But you'll be back to pleasuring the wenches in no time, filling their heads with your blarney heroics." Gabe could feel the healing furrow along his scalp. "Aye," Caleb said. "A close run thing." A bandage was also in place across Gabe's left shoulder and around his waist. Gabe found himself peering at his bandaged body, and then looked beneath the covers. As he did so, Caleb volunteered, "It's naked as a jay bird, you are!" Gabe started to ask who had undressed him, but wasn't able to finish his question as Lady Deborah and Gil had entered the room with Dagan

195

behind them.

"Hungry?" Anthony asked.

Realizing he was, Gabe answered, "Ravenous."

Later that evening, Gabe managed to hobble to a chair on the porch. There was a glint of sunshine still on the horizon. The rain had stopped but the air was still damp. He had closed his eyes, enjoying the peace while the hint of cool breeze blew upon his face. Relaxing so, he sensed another presence. Opening his eyes, Gabe saw Lady Deborah standing there smiling down at him. "It was you who took care of me!" Gabe's comment was more a statement than a question.

"Along with Caleb, Gil, and Dagan," she replied.

"But it was you who cared for me somewhere in those lost days. I can remember soft, gentle hands. It was not unlike Mother's hands when I was a little boy and got hurt."

"It was the least I could do for my future brother-in-law," Deborah replied as she reached down and took Gabe's offered hand. "Gil loves you so much. He was worried sick about you, and yet at the same time was filled with pride at your gallant stand. He has prayed daily for your recovery. He said his life has been much more complete with you in it. He was afraid he'd lose you before the two of you really were able to share time together."

Gabe tried to hide the moisture growing in his eyes. "I too am glad to have discovered my brother. He is so much like father."

Lady Deborah's face creased into a big smile. "Its funny you should say so, because that's exactly what your brother said of you."

Minutes later Dagan stood out from the shadows where he'd been standing, watching and listening. He'd seen the Lady standing by Gabe and pulling his head to her body in a loving, caring manner. Now he felt at peace. "I knew it," he said to himself as he walked down the hill to fetch a wet. It was in the cards. He'd seen it. But watching the Lady with Gabe validated his thoughts. "Boy's got a family and a future jes' like the cards said."

Chapter Seventeen

Anthony and Commodore Gardner were seated at a table overlooking a bustling English Harbour.

"Damn'd lucky I'd say," the Commodore said for the second or third time. They were enjoying a cool glass of lime juice. Anthony watched as the remaining piece of ice was swirled around in the light green liquid. As Gardner drained the glass, he rattled the ice. It was the last of his stores and the commodore seemed to be extracting as much enjoyment as he could before this last sliver was gone. Anthony had found a particle or two of sawdust in his glass but he didn't comment on it, not wanting to interrupt his host. After pacing back and forth in front of the big window, he stuck his fingers in the glass, retrieving the ice and popping it in his mouth, filling the room with a loud crunch. Noticing that Anthony was watching, the commodore said, "I couldn't chew ice not too long ago. A good fellow in the colonies fixed me up with a good pair of choppers and now I can eat what I want. Fellow's from Virginia and said he'd fixed a set for Colonel George Washington. Now

I hear that Washington may lead an army against us." He paused as he heard a rap on the door.

A midshipman entered. "The carriage is ready, sir."

"Very good. Gil, let's be off to see that damn captured slave ship. He was lucky, I tell you. Gabe was just damn lucky," the commodore said again, his mind fixed on Gabe's heroics and wounds.

Lieutenant Pope had been right. The captured vessel had been a slaver in its day. He showed Anthony and Commodore Gardner the ring bolts and chains which were still in place. "I think Bart may have been right when he said 'probably left to hold hostages.'"

Gardner nodded but replied, "As far as we know, there's been no request for ransom as yet."

Anthony agreed but added, "Maybe they've not captured the right person so far. Could be they're waiting for some big political capture or even a high ranking officer."

"Hopefully someone above commodore rank," Gardner added, to which Pope and Anthony had a good laugh.

The slaver was a nimble vessel. She had proved that when she had come about quick as you please and poured a broadside into *Shark*.

"She's a barque. With her sleek lines and finely raked mast I'd say there was a fair amount of American influence involved in her construction, if not American built. She was certainly built as a slaver, otherwise her hull would have been built wider to carry more cargo like the British barques we're used to. She's also got a fair amount of armament," Buck said, joining in the conversation. "Do you think she got those off of captured English ships?"

"I'm not sure," Pope answered. "They would have slowed her down too much when she was being used as a slaver. They were probably added when she turned pirate."

"It's hard to believe there'd be that much more profit in piracy than in slavery," Anthony commented.

"Well sir, only the survivors share the plunder in piracy," Pope stated.

Commodore Gardner had long since placed a handkerchief over his nose. "My God! How'd any of them manage to stand the stench?"

Anthony took a step back from Gardner. After his comment about the smell, Anthony noticed his friend looked pale and ready to spew his lunch. Pope and Buck didn't appear to notice, or chose to ignore Gardner's discomfort.

"The scum we captured were no cleaner than the slaves. No doubt they were as used to the slaves' stench as their own filth," Anthony said.

"Well, filthy or not, they proved to be hard men. Those sixteen twelve-pounders were well manned," Pope volunteered.

"Aye," Buck acknowledged.

Just looking at the *Shark* was proof of that. "I'd like to take those two long nines. They're in better shape than our bow chasers," Buck said, hoping to make a swap for the newer guns.

Anthony nodded, but didn't say anything. No use to create more paperwork when it wasn't necessary. It was sometimes easier to ask forgiveness than to obtain permission.

With all the talk about the guns going on, Pope couldn't help but recall that first onslaught. His body gave an involuntary shudder. "Thank God they were after plunder and not trying to sink us. Otherwise, the lot of us would be goners." Pope put to words what the others were thinking. "Had they known the size of our crew they would have stood off and pounded us into submission or sunk us. We're lucky they were boarding before they realized we were more than a coastal trader."

The battle had become so intense that once the pirates had gotten their blood up they failed to keep a lookout. *Drakkar* and the schooners had arrived before the pirates knew what was happening. One minute they'd all but taken *Shark*. The next they'd been taken themselves.

"The whoresons got what they deserved," Bart commented for the first time. "I lost a few mates among the jack tars and marines they kilt."

Many had died and some were still recovering in the hospital. Anthony found he was glad Gabe had talked him into giving Caleb passage. His skill and help with so many wounded had been invaluable. Kramer was as good as any ship's surgeon, but many would have died waiting on his services had Caleb not been present to help. He'd certainly taken care of Gabe.

As Anthony made to depart with Commodore Gardner, he overheard Dagan making a comment to Bart. "What was that you said?" he asked Dagan.

"I was just commenting on the odd names of the ships we've taken, sir. It seems they've taken on a gruesome tone, so to speak, like the pirates are trying to create fear in the way they've named their ships. We know the big frigate that done for poor Mr. Pitts is *Reaper*. We already took *Rascal* and *Shark*. Now this one is *Scythe*. I can't help but wonder if this is a sign, an omen, if you will."

The men working close by had all stopped their work as they heard Dagan's comments. It had suddenly got very quiet and still. Realizing the effect his words were having on the men and officers before him, Dagan changed his tack. *No use scaring the men*, he thought.

"Yes sir, I do believe its an omen alright, but a bad omen for the bloody buggers who sailed those ships, and its prize money for us. Eh mates?"

That set the men back in good spirits, and they gave a hearty cheer. Anthony was glad Dagan had put a spin on his thoughts for the men's sake, but he agreed. The pirate leader appeared to be doing his best to set an eerie tone to the whole mess. The capture of *Scythe* would certainly add to the men's already fat purses. He wanted them to dwell on that, not fear. They had been lucky so far. While this prize would also help Anthony's purse, what excited him the most was the papers and information they'd discovered. The pirate captain had been so sure of his victory over *Shark* he'd not bothered to take precautions with his papers. Now Anthony had them, and *Scythe's* former captain was shark bait.

The man had obviously been a good seaman and a fearless fighter, but he didn't trust his memory. They had found the answer to the rendezvous puzzle. The man had a chart, and in the margins he had written down dates and numbers. On the charts, numbers were written beside corresponding locations. St. John was number five, St. Kitts was number seven, and St. Lucia was number nine, and so on.

***

ANTHONY'S DINING AREA WAS full of tobacco smoke, the faint but distinct odor of alcoholic spirits, and the unmistakable air of good cheer. All of Anthony's officers had gathered for a council of war. Armed with their latest intelligence, a plan for the *Reaper's* capture or destruction was being carried out. With Pope's knowledge of local waters, Anthony called upon the lieutenant for specific recommendations. The admiralty charts were far from accurate in regards to the specific depths, shoals, and channels around the rendezvous area. This was information Anthony had to have in order for *Drakkar* to be positioned so that she could spring from her hiding place, and close the door on the trap that he was planning for *Reaper*. It had to be a complete surprise to work. Therefore, accurate information had to be obtained. The local charts were more reliable, but a scouting expedition would have to be undertaken before Anthony would feel satisfied.

According to the captured documents, the *Reaper* would rendezvous with *Scythe* on 16 March. If either ship failed to meet on that day, an attempt to rendezvous again would be made on 20 March. The rendezvous would take place at Snake Island. Pope stated that with the tides and season being as they were, he was sure *Reaper* would take the Anegoda Passage. The only piece of the puzzle missing was the time of day the meeting was to occur. Nothing about times had been found, and the pirate captain was dead so he couldn't tell. With Anthony's agreement, Pope had proposed to place one schooner and the ketch between Crab Island and the passage to Puerto Rico. The other two schooners would be placed between Crab Island and St. Croix. *Drakkar* would be anchored in the shallows between Virgin Gorda and St. John Island. That way, *Reaper* would be in the box before anyone knew the difference, if all went as planned. A damned big "IF!"

The problem being that something was always likely to go awry. They may put the tiger in a cage, but she was still a tiger, and dangerous.

"The schooners are no match for *Reaper's* broadside," Anthony cautioned his officers. "*Rascal* is proof of that. I'll not send good men to their death in a useless display of courage. I've no doubt as to your bravery and devotion. If you need to sink the vessel to close off a channel to prevent *Reaper's* escape, so be it. Get the men off, and scuttle the ship where it'll do the most good. Remember floating bodies and wreckage has yet to slow down *Reaper*. Those officers in command will be given written orders. However, I don't want any of this conversation discussed once this meeting is over. I trust each of you, but I'm not yet convinced we don't have a spy in our midst or possibly ashore, slipping information to the cutthroats. If we do, then our plan is all for naught. The bastard will know we've captured *Scythe*, and we'll never see him at the rendezvous point. Am I clear?" All answered in unison. "Well, enough of that then. I know you'll all act honorably. We have two weeks till our first rendezvous is to take place. We'll have plenty of time to carry out our usual patrols and do a little extra scouting of the rendezvous area in order to make any necessary changes. However, all work and no play makes for dull officers. Therefore, as duty allows, let's get cleaned up and make ready for the commodore's festivities this evening. I hear there are ladies who have made their way here from St. Johns just to say they've been in company with some of our randy fellows."

As the officers were making their way out of the dining area, Anthony overheard a story between Markham, Earl, and Gabe. Caleb's damn ape had walked up behind a tavern wench, and while she was serving drinks the ape lifted the back of her skirt, grabbed her thighs, and stuck his hairy head between her legs. The frightened, screaming girl pulled up the front of her skirt only to see the grinning face of the ape that was still holding onto her thighs. Realizing it wasn't a man, but not sure what had a hold of her, she attempted to jump up on one of the benches. With all the screaming and dancing around by the girl, the ape lost his hold on her thighs. Reaching for a new handhold, he grabbed her bloomers. However, with the wench still jumping about these fell down to her ankles, tripping her. There she lay face down on the tavern floor with spilled ale everywhere, and her naked arse shining up like a great moon. The whole tavern was aroar. Caleb had to give the poor ape a whole glass of ale to calm it down after the wench had frightened it so. Markham, Earl, and Gabe were out of the room then, their laughter fading as they headed topside. Anthony and Buck, overwhelmed at what they'd heard, stared at one another.

"The poor ape. What about the wench?" Buck asked.

"Damme, sir, but damme. I don't know," an awed Anthony replied.

***

LADY DEBORAH WAS BEAUTIFUL, dressed in a bare shouldered gown of emerald green, which matched her eyes perfectly. She had noticed Anthony's stare.

"You don't approve?"

"Ah! Au contraire, my darling. If only you knew how magnificent you looked, you'd forgive my stare," Anthony answered as he allowed a lingering gaze at her splendid bosom.

Deborah pretended to be annoyed. She mildly pinched his arm and whispered, "People are watching!"

"Who cares? God gave me eyes so that I may better appreciate the beauty which he created."

Flipping her fan to cover her upper chest, Deborah said, "Look upon, yes. Ogle, no. You were ogling, my dear." She then tried to hide her smile with the fan. Anthony's open admiration was something she'd never experienced in her first marriage. She found herself actually excited that Anthony was so blatant about his feelings and desires. She was glad their engagement was now public knowledge. Not that the entire island hadn't already discussed her love life. She didn't care, but she didn't want Anthony to be upset by the gossip.

"Gabe appears to be healing well. He is his old self again," Deborah commented to change the conversation away from her bosom.

"Yes. Caleb is a fine physician. I question his moral fiber, and worry about his influence on

Gabe and many of my younger officers. But as bad as Caleb is, his ape is worse. Darling, you wouldn't believe the mischief it gets into. It's appalling."

Again Deborah couldn't hide her smile as his comment brought to mind the latest gossip. "I heard about the girl in the tavern."

"You...You've heard?" Anthony was flustered.

"Oh yes. The whole island is discussing it. Greta laughed until she cried when she told me." Trying to control her own laughter, Deborah whispered to Anthony in a husky voice, "I expect I'd holler and scream too if I suddenly found strange hands on my thighs and a hairy head stuck between my legs."

"Deborah! My word, how you talk!"

"Oh hush. Remember that this is a small island starved for excitement or something that will break the monotony. How many tongues do you think you set to wagging, bedding me when I was supposed to be in mourning? Caleb is a good boy. He's just not found the right woman to tame him as of yet. I would gladly ignore his womanizing and pranks to have him caring for my people. As for the monkey, I'll keep my dress down and my legs together."

Commodore Gardner and Greta were approaching so Anthony was unable to respond to Deborah's comments.

"Ah Gil, my friend, how about a glass of hock while it still has a chill on it?" The hock was good.

Noting Anthony's appreciation, Commodore Gardner volunteered, "This is the last of what I got off a merchant from Virginia. He swears it came straight from the Rhine Valley in Hochheim, Germany. It cost a pretty penny but we owe ourselves a few luxuries I'd say; especially since we're stuck out here in the middle of nowhere as we are. Men die young, while women dry up like old prunes."

From the sound of Gardner's conversation he'd had too much of his own hock. Turning toward Deborah, the commodore belched into his fist, and after begging her pardon asked, "Have you had any time with your uh, deceased husband's cousin?"

"Nephew. Gregory's nephew," Lady Deborah corrected.

"Who?" asked Anthony.

"Why Caleb, you silly man. Didn't you know Caleb was coming here to visit Gregory and I? He had not been informed of Gregory's death when the two of you met. Can you guess how shocked he was?" Deborah exclaimed.

It was Anthony who was shocked. No wonder Deborah took up for the man as she had done. "You should have told me," he muttered, feeling somewhat peeved and embarrassed.

Deborah was gently waving her fan, trying to create enough air to prevent her from perspiring. The night was hot enough, but with all the candles burning the heat was rising. She could also feel a touch of heat from Anthony. Realizing she had angered him by failing to tell of her relation to Caleb, she sought to change the subject to something lighter. With a deft movement of her hand she snapped the fan shut and, using it as a pointer, directed everyone's attention across the room. "My, would you look at that?"

Several young ladies, who were making much to do over his recent wounds, had surrounded Gabe. Most were the daughters of local planters and merchants. To them, Gabe would be the perfect catch. A dashing young officer from a well-to-do family, who had already become something of a local hero.

Gabe appeared to be soaking up the attention. His scars seemed to attract more than the usual amount of admiration. For his part, Gabe was doing his best to act the modest, if not reluctant, hero.

"I'd just swoon if I was that age again and a dashing hero like Gabe made eyes at me."

"Hush, Greta! What you'll swoon from is that damn corset if you don't loosen it. You're already turning pink."

The little group laughed at the commodore's remarks to his wife. The ladies then walked outside to talk, and the commodore went to recharge his glass. As Anthony moved to follow Gardner, he glanced back toward Gabe in time to see one young lass touch the almost healed furrow caused by the pistol ball. As she touched the area, she jerked her hand back suddenly and held it to her breast. It was almost like she'd felt the heat from the pistol ball that had torn a path along Gabe's temple to the back of his scalp. Yes, Gabe was soaking it up as he should. But Anthony couldn't help but wonder if Gabe would still be here if the shot had been a little more accurate.

Not one to let their comrade bask in the spotlight by himself, Markham, Earl, and Caleb made their way into the small group. After all, Gabe couldn't handle all these young lasses by himself. He was still healing. Anthony could only imagine the three casting good-natured insults toward Gabe while boastfully bringing attention to their own heroics.

Gardner had returned and offered Anthony a full glass. "What a sight," he said. "What I'd give to be young again."

Greta and Deborah had returned and, hearing her husband's comments, Greta volunteered, "Yes! Young and broke!"

***

AFTER A FULL EVENING of festivities, Anthony and Deborah were waiting on their carriage. Buck approached the two, trying not to show his excessive consumption of the commodore's spirits. Deborah surprised Anthony with her grasp of military lingo, when she exclaimed, "Why Mr. Buck. Are you in your cups?"

"Aye, my lady. It's sorry I am that you've seen me in such a state."

"Well, come on Rupert. We'll give you a ride down to the quay, and a boat will take you to the ship. You may fall overboard and drown, but at least you won't fall and break your neck rolling down the hill."

As Buck was leaving the carriage at the quay, Anthony saw Dagan. He was in conversation with a mulatto woman. She was putting coins in her purse, while Dagan was reaching into a cage and retrieving out a bird, a large, black bird...a raven. Anthony suddenly felt cold. His body gave an involuntary shudder, and a chill went down his spine. His chest felt tight like his breath was suddenly taken away. In his drunken state, Buck, witnessing the action, volunteered, "Looks like Dagan's done got himself a pet bird." Anthony was disturbed; a man didn't purchase a pet bird at two in the morning.

Sounding harsher than he meant to, he said, "*Drakkar's* a warship, not Noah's bloody ark. First Caleb's damn ape and now Dagan's bird." Anthony couldn't explain to Deborah or Buck how uneasy he felt after seeing Dagan with the raven. *They'd just laugh and say I'm superstitious*, he thought. But still the feeling remained, like a phantom in his soul. The old servant's comments were still sharp in Anthony's memory. "'E talks to the ravens, sir. Aye, I've seen him do it."

Chapter Eighteen

THE *SHARK* RETURNED TO English Harbour five days after she'd weighed anchor. Anthony felt an uneasiness lift when the lookout reported *Shark's* sighting. Pope and Gabe would be coming aboard soon with their scouting report, so there was no need to signal "repair on board." For that matter, there was no need for Gabe or Pope to realize how anxious he was to get this rendezvous matter settled.

"Silas!"

"Aye, sir."

"See if you can get a little chill on some of that hock Commodore Gardner gave me. There might be an occasion to broach a bottle."

"They's a couple of bottles in the bilges now, sir. I'm sure they'd be just right for drinkin. I'll go fetch 'em meself, I will." Silas didn't need to be told what the occasion was. He'd heard of *Shark's* sighting like everyone else.

Bart had it right enough when he said, "Cap'n's quite taken with young Mister Anthony." Silas had only seen Admiral Anthony on one occasion, but the young Mister Anthony looked much like him. Could this be the reason for his master's feelings? Bart had also made the comment when Anthony had raised his broad pennant: "Us'll have another Admiral or two in the family, Silas. You just mark me words."

Dagan had agreed saying, "It's so written."

Therefore, as far as Silas was concerned, it was gospel. The only thing that remained was for the correct time to come. Silas never thought to question Dagan about where it was written.

***

IT WAS A BRIGHT day. The predawn overcast had eased, and then was swept inshore by a "goodly breeze." Looking over at *Shark* through his glass, Anthony could make out Nathan Lavery. The midshipman had been spread out among the various ships like everyone else. He was no doubt dreaming of glory and promotion to lieutenant.

"Ready to weigh anchor, sir."

"Very well, Mr. Buck. Get us underway."

As *Drakkar* and her little flotilla beat out of English Harbour, several coastal luggers and the mail packet met them. Anthony was pacing up and down the quarterdeck, deep in thought. No one invaded his private space when he paced. He'd seen the mail packet as did everyone else, but his mind was on the upcoming battle...his appointment with destiny. Would his fate be that of fortune, or would he become infamous? Buck walked to the edge of Anthony's space and waited to be recognized. He would not break Lord Anthony's reverie.

"What's on your mind, Mr. Buck?"

"I was wondering, sir, do you think they'll have mail for us when we return?"

Speaking more harshly than he meant to, Anthony snapped, "Maybe Mr. Buck, for those of us lucky enough to return in one piece."

Buck could see the somber look on Anthony's face, and knew he was worried. He was worried more for those he was going to put in harm's way than for himself. However, he was at a loss for words.

Bart had been standing close and heard the exchange between Anthony and Buck. He knew Buck wanted to say something, but was hesitant, so he volunteered, "Don't ye be worrying, Cap'n. Lady luck is with us. Why it's in the scriptures. Dagan done said so."

"In the scriptures!" Anthony snapped. "Pray tell what chapter and verse, as well as what book would I find this passage?"

"Well sir, if Dagan weren't yonder with Mister Gabe, I'd ask him for you. I surely would. Course if yew's that curious, we could signal and have him come aboard."

"Curious?"

"Aye, sir."

"Why you damned old blackguard. I ought to keelhaul you. Curious, huh!"

Bart turned away, mumbling as he headed toward the companionway. "What was that?" Anthony called. Bart turned back and said, "T'wern't no need trying to hurt me feelings."

Shocked, Anthony said, "Hurt your feelings?"

"Aye, sir. Yew know's we's both be the same age. Ain't no need calling me old."

"Why damme, Mr. Buck, we got us a cheeky shellback who knows his age." Anthony's mood seemed to change as he spoke again, "Maybe Dagan's lady luck is with us, Rupert."

Bart headed back down toward the great cabin. Maybe Silas had put a couple of wets back. Hot as it was getting to be, a wet would go good about now. However, even if Silas didn't have anything put back, he felt better knowing he'd broken "the cap'n's mulligrubs."

***

"IT'S TIME, SIR." BART was standing there. "It's time."

Before Anthony's eyes came to focus, he could smell the coffee and knew Bart had a cup for him.

"Master says we's in for a quick squall, and then it should be fair winds rest of the day." Looking out the stern window, Anthony could see it wasn't dawn yet. Following his gaze, Bart volunteered, "It's about a hour before daybreak."

Anthony still had his uniform on, and now he ached where his coat had gathered under his back. He'd come down to the cabin to get out of the watch's way. He didn't want them to feel his own anxiety and misgivings. He'd sat on the cot, and at some point fell asleep. "Did the men rest?"

"Aye, sir. It was a bit cramped with all the extra

men on board, but they rested. That extra tot of rum you ordered was jes the right thing to help 'em sleep, like little babes at their mama's teats."

Anthony snorted. Where Bart came up with all his little analogies one could only guess. However, they were usually accurate, frequently profane, but accurate. Anthony had commandeered every available man he could from Antigua. A ship the size of the *Reaper* would ordinarily carry a crew of three hundred and fifty or so men. However, being a pirate ship, she may well have five hundred aboard.

When Anthony came on deck he could feel the wind. A quick squall, the master had predicted. The wind caused a flapping noise, possibly where a sail wasn't furled tightly.

"Damme, sir. Take another turn there, would you? Your watch is as loose as a whore's drawers, Mr. Markham. I expected more of you, sir."

"Aye, sir," Markham replied to the first lieutenant. He then called, "Bosun, brail up there if you will. I trust I don't have to remind you of your duties, sir, experienced old salt that you are."

"Aye, Lieutenant. We'll see to it."

"McCarty! You 'eard the lieutenant!"

Anthony smiled to himself. A game! Buck got on Lieutenant Markham, Lieutenant Markham got on the bosun, and the bosun got on the nearest sod who was probably just waking up. The saying 'shat rolls downhill' was certainly true in his Majesty's Navy. It was also apparent that Buck's nerves were worn a bit. The *Scythe* had already anchored off Snake Island. In the distance, a few lights were visible, possibly Snake Island or St. Thomas. Lights on Virgin Gorda, St. John, and Tortola were in sight as well.

Anthony had sent a party ashore under cover of darkness, and had them cut a few fronds and tops out of palm trees. He then had the carpenter and his mates attach the tops to planks that could easily be discarded when needed. Until then they were fixed to the mast, yardarms, and along the rail. This would help disguise the ship's appearance. While it might not stand close scrutiny, *Drakkar* would be hard to pick out at first glance, nestled in a small inlet as she was.

Drakkar had dropped her anchor as close to shore as possible between St. John and Virgin Gorda. "Too damn close for my liking," the master had said. If the approaching squall had any force they'd have to get underway, and that would ruin all of Anthony's plans. Yet he could understand the master's apprehension. When the wind died down, one could hear the surf. Fortunately, the wind was now coming from the north-northeast. While Anthony couldn't see them, he knew the ketch and schooners would be in place. Now it was a waiting game. Hurry the hell up...and then wait. Buck, Peckham, the gunner, and the bosun were all in conversation when a member of the watch nudged Lieutenant Markham. Still smarting from the first lieutenant's remarks about a loose watch, Markham greeted Anthony without informing Buck that he was present.

"Good morning, sir. It will be light soon. I've kept a watch on the anchors and we've not drifted."

Peeved, Buck turned and greeted Anthony. "Promises to be a warm one by mid morning," Peckham volunteered.

"Ah, but the question is for whom," Anthony replied. Turning to Buck, he said, "Put your best eyes aloft today. I want good men with a glass at the masthead and change them every two hours."

"Aye, aye, sir." Buck had already taken care of the lookouts, but it didn't hurt for Anthony to remind him. Another little breeze caused a small flapping noise overhead. The group looked up as one. Anthony's broad pennant.

Funny, Anthony thought. He hadn't even thought about that for some time, hadn't even really considered himself a commodore. Bart had yet to address him as anything other than "Cap'n" or sir. However, there flapping in the wind was his proof. There was the pennant that men would follow into battle this day. Some would die; maybe he'd die. *God be with Gabe,* he suddenly prayed.

Buck had followed Anthony's gaze. "She makes a pretty sight, doesn't she, sir?"

"Yes, Mr. Buck. That she does."

"I hope you don't mind my saying so, sir, but I think the Admiralty did the right thing giving you the broad pennant. I just wish you could have had a true flag captain."

Without knowing it, Buck had touched on Anthony's feelings. If he'd had a flag captain, maybe he would have felt more like a commodore. "Well, Mr. Buck," Anthony answered, "Let's just be thankful for the support they did give us, and let us not be forgetting all the help Commodore Gardner has been."

"Aye, sir. A great help he's been too."

Silas peered above the companionway. "Are you ready for your breakfast, sir?" Seeing Anthony's look, Silas added, "We've got butter and jelly to go on some bread. That'd go good with a fresh cup of coffee if ya want something light."

"Sounds good, Silas. I'll be down directly. Have the men been fed, Mr. Buck?"

"Aye, sir, and we're ready to go to quarters."

"I shall break my fast then."

At that moment, from above, came the whispered cry, "Deck there. Sail to the nor-east." Even though Anthony had been expecting the sighting to be sooner than later, he was startled at the cry. He was suddenly apprehensive. He could second-guess all his plans if he wanted, but that wouldn't change a thing. Today would be a day of reckoning!

"She's coming down the passage just like Pope predicted," Buck was saying.

"Aye, but a bit early, I'm thinking," Anthony replied.

"Better to get it over with," Peckham chimed

in.

"It'll be a while yet," Anthony said looking at his watch. "I shall have my breakfast, I think. Bart!"

"Here, sir."

"Let's go eat."

"Aye, aye, sir."

As the commodore and his cox'n disappeared, Peckham asked Davy, "Well young sir, have you ever seen such a cool 'un?"

"No, sir," Davy said, still in awe. Standing at the foot of the mainmast, the bosun had seen and heard the entire conversation. As he moved forward he recalled his recent conversation with Bart about being part of Anthony's family. "Reckon the sod is family," he muttered to himself, "eating breakfast with 'is lordship and the like."

***

When Anthony returned back on deck he was patting his stomach. "Nothing gets a man ready for battle like a full belly, Rupert."

Buck, hearing Anthony, turned and replied, "Aye, that it does, sir. But if you get a belly full of lead its an agonizing death, I'm told."

"Well, thank you very much for your insight, Lieutenant," Anthony replied. "Just what I wanted to hear!"

"It's light enough now, sir," Buck continued, ignoring Anthony's sarcasm. "The lookouts have made out two different ships."

"Two?" Anthony said, alarmed.

"Aye, sir. One is definitely the *Reaper*, and the other is a smaller ship, possibly a brig. Maybe a captured vessel."

"We've not been sighted?" Anthony questioned.

"There's been no sign we have, sir. But without expecting us and with the way you've got us camouflaged we'd be hard to spot."

Anthony nodded. *Drakkar* would be hard to spot. But if she were, she'd be like a sitting duck for awhile. However, with the sun rising and the islands lying behind them, the ship was hidden as well as a ship could be. But two ships! They were expecting the *Reaper*-not the *Reaper* and another ship. No plans were made to take on two pirates. There had been many questions left unanswered, and one wouldn't have to look far to find flaws in this plan. He should have considered *Reaper* might well have been rendezvousing with more than one ship. "Damme," he said out loud. It would be a hellish job taking on *Reaper* by herself, but now the odds looked insurmountable.

Buck volunteered again, seeing the concern on Anthony's face. "The brig's not flying a flag, sir, so she may be a taken ship."

"Took or not, Mr. Buck, she's crewed by a band of cutthroats that'll know how to use her better than the crew she sailed with most likely."

Reaper was at that moment passing to windward of where *Drakkar* lay in wait. Anthony felt a queasy sensation in his stomach. He felt almost naked watching as *Reaper* passed. A look-out called down in a voice just loud enough to be heard: "She got a vice admiral's flag flying, sir."

"Damned cheekish if you ask me," Buck declared, looking through a ship's glass. Anthony took his own glass and peered. Sure enough, a vice admiral's flag flew at the foremast.

"Bloody ass," Peckham chimed in. "It's no small wonder 'e ain't flying an admiral of the fleet's flag."

"Impertinent, he may be," Anthony said. "But he's already partially succeeded in his goal for flying that rag."

Buck and Peckham gave Anthony a questioning look. "He's already got your British blood boiling. You're stirred up and angry."

"Angry men rush in where wise ones would tread softly, gentlemen. We are outmanned and outgunned. To see this day through we must keep our wits about us."

Turning back toward *Reaper*, Anthony couldn't help but admire her. Foe she may be, but she presented a proud sight. Proud and deadly. Anthony could still envision her swift attack on *Rascal*. He would never forget Merle Pitts' words, "I wanted you to be proud." *Reaper* remained close-hauled on her present tack.

"She's taking in her main course, sir," Peckham said. "Looks like top gallant's already brailed up."

"Think they've already sighted *Scythe*, sir?" Buck asked.

"If not, they're blind or drunk," Anthony replied. Anthony had not misjudged his timing, but how long would it be before that son-o-Satan realized something was amiss? Anchored as she was, *Scythe* was a sitting duck. Anthony could only imagine what a state of nerves Pope and *Scythe's* crew must be under. Most would remember what happened to *Rascal*.

Chapter Nineteen

"CAST OFF OUR DISGUISE if you will, Mr. Buck, and prepare to get underway. I don't want to be late for this engagement."

"Aye, sir. Mr. MacMorgan, if you'd be so kind as to get these laggards busy, I'd appreciate it. It's time to show that snail eating sodomite that *Drakkar's* a warship and not a fooking jungle."

MacMorgan smiled to himself as he got the men busy with the help of some of his mates. Mr. Buck was getting his dander up. He only talked like that when the 'shat was about to go splat'. MacMorgan just hoped not too much splatted on him.

Anthony found himself pacing the quarter-deck. Buck didn't need him interfering with getting the ship underway.

Pope, on board the *Scythe*, was to let loose a broadside into the *Reaper* at the most opportune time. But when exactly was that? Anthony was confident Pope would judge it right. He had commanded a brig before becoming first lieutenant on a first rate flag ship. He had the experience, but that didn't curtail Anthony's worry.

If they fired too soon, *Reaper* would stand off

and let loose her own devastating broadside that would end the show before it began. If they waited too late then they'd be overrun before *Drakkar* and the schooners could assist.

The big question right now was the brig. How was she armed and how many men did she have on board? Were there any prisoners on board that could be freed and help in the fight? Anthony gazed about him. Mr. Davy stood by the mainmast, laying a hand to discarding *Drakkar's* camouflage. He still looked youthful, but different than the snit that had faced Witzenfeld with such tenacity. Seasoned. That was the difference. He was now a seasoned veteran who had seen more action than some sitting behind a desk at Whitehall. Would he still look youthful tomorrow? Would he even be alive tomorrow? Anthony couldn't help but feel the burden as he placed young Davy and all the others in his flotilla in harm's way. Duty! Damme, if that wasn't a fine word at Whitehall. But most of these men could care less than a fiddler's fart about duty. It was their mates and the ship, and to hell with the rest of it.

"We're ready to get underway, sir. The anchor's hove short."

"Very well, Mr. Buck. Proceed, but do it quietly. I feel the trap is already set, but let us not tip our hand till Pope has had his say."

"Aye, sir," Buck replied, grinning at Anthony's word. "Pope will let his cannons do his talking, and by gawd I hope he kills that Frenchman with his first words."

Anthony could feel *Drakkar* come alive and make headway. Picking up a breeze, her sails filled and grew taut.

"Mr. Peckham!"

"Aye, sir!"

"Lay us alongside that French bastard yonder, and let's hope *Scythe* has left a piece of dessert for our troubles."

"Aye, sir. Dessert we'll have if I'm any judge."

***

"Deck there. Looks like *Reaper's* dropping her anchor, sir." No sooner had the lookout hailed down when the sound of thunder filled the air. *Scythe* had let loose her broadside. Each cannon was loaded with grape on top of ball.

"Cut it close he did," Peckham remarked.

"Well, it don't matter much now if 'e see's us do it, Cap'n, the sods bound to know sumthin's amiss."

"Well, damme Bart," Anthony said. "Where did you come from? I'd begun to wonder if you'd taken leg bail."

"Leg bail, why no sirree. If I was to do that, who'd see to getting my betters out o' the trouble they's always getting into?"

Bart was right. However, rushing down under full sail, only a blind man would miss *Drakkar* with her dragon figure head looking defiant and warning all.

Pope had let loose another broadside. Mr. Davy had climbed up on the bulwark for a better view.

"Caught him flat-footed, sir. That damned pirate ain't even fired a musket in return yet."

"Taken to cussin a wee bit, have we, young sir?" Bart asked Davy.

"Er, sorry sir. I was just caught up in the excitement."

"Apology accepted, Mr. Davy," Anthony replied, trying to hide his smile.

"Deck there!" hailed the mast head lookout. "The brig is tacking and opening her gun ports, sir."

Scythe's broadside had created so much smoke the brig's actions were obscured from *Drakkar's* quarterdeck.

"Does that answer your questions about the brig, Mr. Buck?"

"Aye, it does, sir. I bet the frog thinks he's outta deep shat now, but he's in error, I'm thinking."

The wind had cleared most of the smoke, and the brig was visible again. "She's shaking out her topsails," Peckham said. "Looks like she intends to cross *Scythe's* stern and lay a broadside up her arse end."

Anthony could only clench and unclench his fists. The lookout called down again, "*Shark* and *Rascal's* beating down on the brig, sir."

"Damme, if I don't feel like climbing up there with him. He's got the best view," Anthony swore.

"Careful now, sir," Bart replied. "Yew ain't as used to them heights as yew used to be. Better to let the yonkers like Mr. Davy do the skylarkin'."

"Damn you, Bart," Anthony replied. "You go too far at times."

"Mr. Buck!"

"Aye, sir!"

"I'd be obliged if after we're finished with this frog you'd be kind enough to explain proper etiquette to Bart before you keelhaul him. Then find me a suitable cox'n — one that will mind his betters and his manners."

"Aye, sir. I'll take care of it directly." Buck had been with Anthony long enough to know the banter between him and the cox'n was to keep the men's minds on them and off the impending battle. It would do no good for the men to get a case of nerves at this point in the game.

The lookout was calling down again, "The brig done gave *Scythe* an arse full sir, but *Shark* has fired and took down the brig's top gallant."

"Maybe that will slow them down some," Buck said.

Smoke again had obscured all vision of the fighting ships. When the wind had finally cleared the smoke, it did little to help Anthony's apprehension. *Reaper* had cut her cable and drifted into *Scythe*. Anthony couldn't help but wonder who had hemmed who in. *Scythe* was certainly in a hellish way. Thunder again filled the air as the brig and *Reaper* fired their cannons into *Scythe*.

"Mr. Buck!"

"Aye, sir."

"I know we're at an extreme range, but I want a broadside poured into that ship. Have Williams lay each gun himself if need be, and fire at will. I want our presence felt now! I'll not see Pope sacrificed like Pitts without firing a shot."

"Aye, sir. I'll tend to it directly."

Drakkar's heavy cannons filled the air with a deafening thunder. Williams must have been waiting, anticipating Anthony's order. "That'll waken the frog eating son-o-bitches," Williams remarked to his gun crews. "Let 'em chew on them balls awhile."

Drakkar's weight rained down on the pirates. Not every ball struck, but those that did left a path of destruction not unlike a hurricane-ripping through sail, severing riggings and cordage, tearing chunks out of the mast, ripping up planking, and creating great gashes in the bulwark as the balls plowed into the deck. The pirates had not met a foe of *Drakkar's* mettle that could wreak so much havoc with a single broadside.

"Another if you please, Mr. Williams," Anthony ordered. "That was music to my ears."

"Aye, sir. On its way," the big gunner replied. "Come on, lads. Let's give 'em another taste with 'is Lordship's blessings. And if they's still not satisfied, we'll give 'em an encore."

Anthony turned to Buck, "After the next broadside, shorten all sail."

"Aye, sir."

"Mr. Peckham. Be so kind as to lay us alongside there if you please," Anthony said, using his sword as a pointer.

"Aye, sir. Alongside she'll be."

Even though every jack tar was expecting it, men jumped as another of *Drakkar's* broadsides were loosened. Double shotted and filled with grape for extra measure. The heavy loads caused *Drakkar* to shudder as she spit forth her authority. The distance was much closer now, and *Drakkar's* path of destruction was obvious.

Anthony called for Lieutenant Dunn. "Here sir!" Dunn reported, his uniform bright and shiny as if he were about to go on parade.

"I'd be obliged if you'd get your sharpshooters stationed where they'd do the most good. I want you to direct their fire toward anyone manning a gun, and then any apparent officer, then any target of choice."

"Aye, sir," Dunn responded. "We'll make their life hell on earth before they reach Hades."

"Mr. MacMorgan!"

"Aye," the bosun hurried over.

"Rig your nets. I don't expect boarders cause I intend to board *Reaper*. But we'd better by prepared anyway." Anthony then took time to look about him.

After *Drakkar's* broadsides, the *Reaper* did look grim all right, but he could see a few cannon barrels poking out of gun ports.

"Mr. Buck!" Anthony shouted. "Everyone down!"

Reaper let loose with the few guns she had left serviceable. The guns fired unevenly, yet many of the balls found their marks. Men were down everywhere. A gun captain was thrashing violently as blood spurted from an open artery where his leg had been. Part of the wheel was shot away. A master's mate had a huge splinter sticking through his neck and blood gurgled as he coughed. Another seaman ran screaming, his hand holding a face that was now a bloody mask. More thuds were felt as some of *Reaper's* balls were hitting between wind and water. Still, Williams and Lieutenant Markham had *Drakkar's* gunners working feverishly.

"Stop your vents! Sponge out! That's it, men. Now load! Be patient and wait for the officers command to fire, me lads! On the up roll. Fire!" The gun crews were tiring, but their work here was almost done.

"Lieutenant Markham! One more broadside, and then you and Mr. Williams split the men into two different boarding parties. You take your men aft, and Williams take his forward. Arm them and await my signal."

"Aye, sir. One more for luck, and then we'll divide up."

"All right lads," Williams called. "You heard 'is Lordship. One more dose and then we'll run through 'em."

The crews were yelling and cursing, but ready. *Drakkar's* next broadside was loosed at point blank range. Williams took time to peer through a gun port and admire the handiwork of his beauties. A goodly portion of *Reaper's* side was destroyed. Not one of her guns was left intact on the larboard side.

"All right now, lads. Our work here is done. Let's go be helping out our mates," Williams yelled. "Half of you go with Lieutenant Markham and t'other half with me."

Lieutenant Markham was not sure he liked the gunner throwing orders about, but he wasn't about to argue with him at this moment.

After *Drakkar's* last salvo the two ships drifted together, the hulls making a grinding noise. Anthony heard the lookout calling down again, "*Shark* and *Rascal* has boarded the brig, sir."

"Buck!"

"Here, sir," he answered, hearing Anthony's call above the increasing din of battle.

"Have Lieutenant Dunn and his marines join Lieutenant Markham's party aft and board *Reaper* by the stern. Gabe and Earl have boarded the brig, and the sight of your party on *Reaper's* stern may help turn the tide."

"Aye, aye sir. We'll handle the bastards."

"Good. Now before you board, make sure the bosun has us grappled together tight. I don't want us drifting apart and the bastard escaping somehow."

"Nay, sir. He'll not get away!"

"Rupert!"

"Sir!"

"It's fight to the finish I'm afraid. There will be no quarter."

"I wouldn't want it any other way, sir." Then Buck was gone.

"Mister Peckham!"

"Aye, sir!"

"I don't feel we'll need you at the wheel for awhile. If you'll get your mates together along with the extra men, we'll board amidships."

"Aye, sir. Let's go men. There's bloody work to be done this day, I'm thinking," the old master shouted to his mates.

Chapter Twenty

DUNN'S SHARPSHOOTERS WERE DOING their part well, but damned if the pirates hadn't gotten men into the rigging. They were marking down men in Anthony's party. As the ocean's swell ground the two hulls together, the yardarms and riggings became tangled. Half blinded by residual smoke from *Drakkar's* last broadside, Anthony gave the signal. Williams's party boarded forward, Buck's party aft, and Anthony's amidships. The pirate captain was momentarily visible to Anthony, but quickly disappeared into a group of fighting men. The sight on board *Reaper* was indeed gruesome. Anthony had never seen such havoc as had been rent by *Drakkar's* gunnery. Guns were upended, carriages lay in splinters, and men lay crushed by the upended cannons, or torn apart like disposed rubbish.

Many of *Drakkar's* balls had plowed a path of destruction from one bulwark clear to the other side. Wounded men were being ignored as their mates were fighting for their lives. Screams and curses filled the air now that the great guns were silent. Pistol and musket shots still rang out. Spent balls thudded into the deck, as more members of Anthony's party were falling prey to the pirates' muskets. A mild breeze was now carrying away the smoke that had helped *Drakkar* by reducing visibility. As they boarded *Reaper*, Anthony heard a loud crack, and then a shout of warning. He turned away just in time to avoid being trapped by more damaged rigging and falling spars. Thankfully most of it fell on a group of pirates. More canvas and cordage were hanging like great obstacles, and men had to hack their way through to fight each other. A bosun's mate with a group of men hurried past Anthony, swinging axes and cutlasses. They shouted insults to the pirates, their arms waving metal blades that shined in the sunlight only to turn dark with blood. Anthony found himself hoarse from shouting encouragement and commands to his men. His earlier apprehensions had given way to a reckless blood lust. Splinters whipped past him, and a few stung his cheek as a pistol ball ricocheted off a downed spar next to him. Anthony turned toward the direction from which the shot had been fired. There was *Reaper's* captain again, smoking pistol in hand. A loud cheer distracted Anthony. Turning, he spied Mr. Davy. Anthony could see tears — fighting tears, mad tears. The boy was giving his all. As Davy wiped away the tears, his face was left streaked with smoke, blood, and grime.

"They've taken the brig, sir," he reported. It was then that Anthony realized Davy was holding his side. A large splinter was protruding where it had embedded along the rib cage. Davy's hand was soaked from blood. Seeing Anthony's gaze, Davy said, "It hurts too much to pull out, sir. I tried."

Anthony turned to Bart. "Get him back to the ship so the surgeon can tend to him."

"But sir, my place is with you."

Anthony was moved by Bart's sincerity, but didn't have time to debate. "Bart!"

"I understands, sir. Come along, young sir. Let's get you back to ole *Drakky* and see if the surgeon might find a wee potion for yer pain."

Anthony turned his attention back to the fight. The pirates were being beaten. Slowly and at a great price — but they were being beaten. The ship was a crazed den of slaughter. A petty officer that was firing a swivel gun suddenly grasped his face and fell headlong between the two ships. A huge pirate swung a blade big as a claymore and beheaded a seaman only to have the man's mate skewer him through the neck, creating a fountain of blood from a severed artery. Men were hacking, stabbing, and slashing at each other.

Anthony thrust his sword into a pirate who was aiming his pistol at a marine. Out of the corner of his eye, Anthony could see Buck, Gabe, and a number of men making their way through the remaining pirates by *Reaper's* stern. Another pirate lunged at Anthony, his eyes glazed, oblivious to his many wounds, but now weakened. Anthony struck him down after a brief parry.

Damme, he thought. *It is still a wee bit hot for my taste.* He was tiring fast, the adrenaline rush was gone. A seaman fell beside him. His eyes were suddenly lifeless and staring into space, a large cutlass embedded in his chest. Without thinking, Anthony quickly dispatched the rogue who had just slain the seaman. Another blade slashed at him then, which he quickly fended off. There face to face and blade to blade, Anthony faced the pirate captain.

Their blades clashed and parted. A feint. A parry. The foes circled, each exploring for the other's weakness warily. Both men were fatigued and were gasping for breath. Their strength was ebbing, but neither was willing to surrender.

Most of the other fighting had now subsided. Buck and Gabe had both reached the outer part of a circle where Anthony and the pirate were dueling. Bart had returned and was almost to the inside of the circle. Sensing a distraction, the pirate lunged, the tip of his sword nicking Anthony's side. Anthony parried the lunge and opened up the pirate's arm from the elbow to the armpit. The arm was all but useless, and blood dripped down the man's sleeve and off the hilt of his sword. Again the pirate lunged. This time Anthony side-stepped and brought his blade down across his opponent's shoulder and collarbone. However, Anthony's arm had grown tired, weak from the prolonged battle. The blade did not strike true. The pirate caught more of the flat side of the blade than the edge. Even with the glancing blow, a large gash was made and more blood began to flow.

"Give!" Anthony cried. "Give!" Then something struck Anthony in the head from behind. He felt himself beginning to fall. His eyes wouldn't focus, and he could feel warm blood running down his neck. He seemed to take forever to fall. As he hit the deck, he felt the pain. He tried to rise but he had fallen in a bloody pool. As he tried pushing himself up, his hands slipped from under him. Anthony felt pain again as someone stood over him and viciously grabbed him by his hair, jerked back his head, and placed a sharp menacing blade at his exposed throat. The pain in his head was terrible, but helped Anthony to refocus. A dead pirate lay next to where Anthony had just risen. Bart's knife was stuck in the fellow's neck. The rogue had apparently struck Anthony from behind and Bart had quickly dispatched him for his troubles. However, the pirate captain was now holding a blade beneath Anthony's chin. He was threatening to sever Anthony's windpipe if he was not given clear passage along with his surviving cohorts.

"No!" Anthony tried to speak out, only to feel a slight burning sensation, and then warm blood trickle down on to his chest. The pirate captain meant business.

"*Rapidement*," he threatened, "Or monsieur will die." The silence was eerie as everyone lowered their weapons and absorbed what was happening. A heavy groan emerged as another swell caused the hulls of the wounded ships to rub together. The groan was haunting. A cloud suddenly darkened the ship, creating shadows.

"*Tu comprends*? You have but a moment, then he dies," the pirate threatened. Buck cleared his throat and started toward the pirate, but Dagan reached out to still him.

"*Diable!*" Dagan shouted to get the pirate's attention. "I am Dagan, sorcerer of Ravennetus. I am the revenger, *corbeau*." Now Dagan's voice was barely audible, not much more than a whisper. However, his words seemed to hypnotize the pirate leader. "Give me the knife. You have no need of such a heavy blade. Enough blood has been spilled today. Surely you've grown tired. It's time to cool your blood and cleanse your tormented soul."

As if in a trance, the pirate captain started to rise, loosening his grip on Anthony as he did so. He appeared to relax as he focused on Dagan. Suddenly the silence was broken as one of the cutthroats screamed, "Cut 'is throat. Kill 'im, Capitaine. Kill 'im." The French captain shook his head as if clearing himself from a daze. The spell had been broken. He jerked Anthony's head back, once again raising his hand with the knife.

"*Au revoir*," he said.

It was then that Dagan raised his head toward the sky and cried out, *"Corbeau attaque Le Diable!"* No sooner had Dagan given his command than a blur of black wings flew down from above, screeching as it did so. The screeching caused the pirate to look up. His doing so provided the attacking bird with a perfect target. The pirate's screams were intermingled with the great bird's flapping wings and screeching. The bird's claws and beak tore chunks of flesh from the pirate's face. The pirate tried to protect his face and eyes with one hand, and fend off the demon bird with the other. But it was no use. The fierce attack had already reduced the pirate's face to a mass of gore, making it hard to recognize as being human.

Anthony was forgotten as the knife was dropped to the deck. The pirate had one eye torn from its socket and was screaming in pain. His arms were thrashing as he tried to combat his tormentor. Back he went. Back as the men moved out of his way, watching in awe at the spectacle that was taking place before them. The bird momentarily ceased his attack as the now blinded Frenchman had backed all the way to the aft rail. The raven's beak and claws had turned red with dripping blood. The bird appeared to hover in the air above the pirate, flapping its wings in an accelerating fashion. The bird then dove at the man's face with such force he toppled over the rail. The pirate had at last grabbed hold of his tormentor, and together they hit the water. The warm Caribbean choked off the anguished screams of the pirate captain and the screeching bird. Once again everything was silent. Slowly the clouds moved, and the sun again shone bright.

Chapter Twenty-One

ANTHONY ROSE FROM WHERE he'd been kneeling on the deck. Touching his neck, he found the bleeding had stopped and the blood had dried. Everyone surrounded him then: Gabe, Bart, Buck, Pope, and Dagan. They were all there. Dagan looked ashen and clammy. His breathing seemed labored. Anthony took his hand and the two looked directly at each other, but no words were spoken. None were needed. When Anthony released his hand, Dagan said, "I think I'll go have a wet." Gabe watched as Dagan made his way toward the *Shark*. He couldn't understand fully what had just transpired, but its effect on Dagan was obvious. He looked drained and weak. Gabe had never seen him like this before. However, but for Dagan's actions, Gabe was sure his brother would be dead now.

Buck looked at Anthony and said, "We've called for the surgeon, sir."

Caleb examined Anthony's wounds and found numerous superficial cuts and bruises. The cut made by the dead pirate captain had been only deep enough to draw blood but nothing else.

That it was superficial did nothing to lessen the menace of the razor sharp blade. It was still fresh in Anthony's memory. The lump on the back of his head was another story. Anthony's scalp was split and would require stitches. The collection of blood under the scalp hurt like hell. It was already so big Anthony couldn't put on his hat.

"Sir! Here, sir!" Buck finally got Anthony's attention. "Are you well enough to move, sir? This ship is taking on water fast and is in danger of sinking."

"Aye, Mr. Buck. Have our wounded removed to *Drakkar* and then conduct a quick search of this vessel if conditions permit."

"Aye, sir," Buck replied as he turned away and set working parties about their assigned duties.

***

ANTHONY WENT WITH GABE, Pope, Bart, and a bosun's mate to make a quick search of the pirate captain's cabin. Bart quickly found a small chest of mixed coins, gold, silver and odd pieces of jewelry. "No doubt some o' 'is plunder 'e's tucked away, I'm thinking," Bart volunteered.

Pope found some papers in a locked desk drawer that seemed to identify the pirate. Old official dispatches and letters were addressed to Capitaine de fre'gate Phillipe Jabot. This proved the rogue had at least been a French naval officer at some point. However, there was nothing to prove the French knew about or sanctioned the piracy Jabot had recently been involved in. Just a man gone bad they'd say. An embarrassment yes, but no official connection to the French government. Anthony and his group searched as long as they dared, but were unable to find anything that would connect a spy to Jabot's operation. Nevertheless, Anthony was certain somebody with a high degree of knowledge of ships' cargoes, passengers, and sailing times had been feeding information to the pirates. Well, no matter. For now it was over.

Once on deck the bosun reported, "The *Scythe* is in a bad way, sir. She's in danger of foundering. The carpenter and his mates are aboard her now."

"All right," Anthony replied, looking about him. He was surprised to see how much the *Reaper* had settled during his quick search of Jabot's cabin. Suddenly, a loud snap resounded, followed by another. Bart, suddenly alarmed, looked at Anthony and said, "Grapnel lines be parting, sir."

"Yes. Let's repair on board *Drakkar*," Anthony replied. Loudly he ordered, "Clear ship! Clear ship!"

When the last man was back on *Drakkar*, Anthony ordered the remaining grapples to be cut. Once the order was carried out, *Drakkar* seem to rise up from her larboard list. *Reaper's* main deck was almost immediately awash. Peckham had moved up to Anthony's side to peer at *Reaper's* demise. Noticing him Anthony said, "I wish Merle Pitts was here to see this."

Tearfully the old master replied, "He does,

sir. I feel it in me soul, he does." Then quietly the once proud ship was gone.

***

IT WAS ONLY AFTER things had settled down that Anthony found out Kramer was dead. Not killed in battle, but at the surgeon's table. A surgeon's mate said he'd just removed a man's leg, took a step back, wiped his brow, and then slid down on the deck lifeless. With Kramer gone, Caleb had once again showed his worth caring for the wounded. Anthony entered the sick berth and almost vomited. The stench of blood and human waste was overpowering. "Excuse me, sir," a loblolly boy said as he sped to the upper deck to empty his full tub of "wings and limbs."

The Reaper is gone, but what a terrible price. All the dead and wounded, Lieutenant Mainard among them. The Admiralty would think it a small price to pay for their victory, Anthony thought as he tried to control his nausea. He spoke to the wounded men and praised them for their gallant efforts. He made his way to Caleb, who had beckoned him over to speak to Mr. Davy.

"The splinter," Caleb explained, "Lies superior to the thorax, sir." Seeing Anthony's puzzled look, Caleb explained further. "The splinter has lodged itself beneath the tissues along Mr. Davy's side, but above the rib cage. Therefore, none of the vital organs that lie within the thorax — er... the chest — are likely to be damaged."

After giving Davy a liberal drink of rum and

placing a leather strap between his teeth, two surgeon's mates held Davy down. Another surgeon's mate handed Caleb a scalpel and a relatively clean cloth to wipe away the blood. Caleb took the scalpel and ran it down the length of the splinter, opening the tissues so that the jagged splinter was plucked from the wound. The doctor then poured a liberal splash of rum over the open tissue to wash away any remnants.

Looking up from his handiwork, Caleb explained to Anthony. "It's better to open such a wound and remove any fragments. Simply extracting the splinter would surely be just as painful. Any fragments not removed would later suppurate, creating a gaseous humour and mortification."

Turning back to his present work, Caleb splashed more rum over the wound and sewed it up leaving an opening with a wick to be drawn out at intervals. Davy had gritted his teeth but never cried out. "Now young sir," Caleb declared, "you'll have every young lass at English Harbour swooning over you. But be warned. Don't over do it, else Lieutenant Anthony may become jealous." Everyone laughed at Caleb's attempt to cheer up the brave boy.

Part III

Voices from the Deep

Last night a voice called to me
So I got up, walked to the beach
The wind did howl, the waves crashed in
I thought about the countless men
Who died trying to keep the ship afloat
The cries I hear is their ghost.

He waved goodbye when they set sail
Got caught up in a fearsome gale.
Sometimes the sea demands a price;
Another sailor gives up his life
He joins his mate in a watery grave
I hear their voices calling to be saved.

So blow, blow
You wind and you rain
A lee shore or a hurricane
Will the ship take the strain?
Or is it going down?
Will another sailor drown

...Michael Aye

Chapter Twenty-Two

ENGLISH HARBOUR WAS ASTIR when *Drakkar* returned with her little flotilla. They were scarred, but victorious.

Much to everyone's surprise, *Scythe* made the trip back. *Drakkar's* carpenter and his mates had been able to staunch the flow of incoming seawater by fothering a doubled up, tar-soaked topsail. Once the canvas patch was in place, the prisoners were put on the pumps to keep the water level down. The majority of *Scythe's* other damage was between wind and water. The pumps were manned watch-and-watch at first. But by the time Antigua was sighted, the pumps only had to be manned one hour in four. Mr. Stokes, the carpenter, had predicted *Scythe* could be completely repaired and declared seaworthy in no time at all.

Commodore Gardner was all nerves and apprehension. From the time Anthony's ships had been sighted it seemed to have taken an eternity for them to beat into the harbour. However, *Drakkar* now stood bows-on to the land. Unable to curb his impatience, Gardner had taken a guard boat out to meet Anthony, appearances be damned.

Now he sat silently, absently drinking a glass of claret, but never tasting it. He was totally engrossed in Anthony's report.

The dialogue was eventually interrupted by a knock on the door. The sentry announced, "Midshipman Young, sir." The lad entered the cabin and seemed to wilt from Commodore Gardner's glare. His anger at having Anthony's narrative interrupted was not lost on the boy.

"Well, don't just stand there. Spit it out, man."

"Er, Mr. Buck's compliments, sir. We're about ready to drop anchor."

"Very well," Anthony replied. "Tell Mr. Buck I'll be on deck directly."

"Aye, sir." The lad then scampered out of the cabin, glad to be out from under Gardner's glare.

"Damn whelp," Gardner remarked. "Well, duty calls, and I've kept you too long, Gil. But damme man, it sounds like you took care of the swines proper like. Here's my hand and congratulations. The island is a buzz from here to St. Johns and back already. Every planter on the island will want to give you a reception to celebrate and share in your glory. Don't know that I envy you there."

***

LADY DEBORAH'S CARRIAGE WAS waiting at the jetty when Anthony finally made it ashore. He climbed in beside her and almost collapsed. She pulled him to her and listened attentively as Anthony summarized the events surrounding the battle.

He then told her if it were not for Dagan he'd be dead. "You would not believe the control he had over Jabot, till some damn rogue broke the trance. Dagan then called down the raven. Where it had been lurking I don't know. I do know I owe Dagan my life." Turning and looking into his woman's eyes Anthony said, "The only thing going through my mind when the blade was at my throat was that you were going to be widowed again, even before we married."

"Oh, darling," Deborah responded as she pulled Anthony to her breast and held him close. "What would I do without you?" Sensing her man's needs, the carriage ride to the cottage had been made in silence with the two holding each other. Anthony could sense a renewal in his body and soul that seemed to come with the closeness of Deborah's body next to his. He could feel her heartbeat as his head lay upon her breast, and he seemed to breathe the very air she breathed. The breath of life.

Just before they arrived at the cottage Deborah sat up. "We have company, dear."

"Company?"

"Yes! And now that you're back we'll have to open up the big house. Our little love nest is too small for everyone."

"Who's here?" Anthony asked.

"Your family, you silly man. They arrived just

as you left. Your sister has been helping with our wedding plans."

"Oh," groaned Anthony. He then said, "Our wedding's still a month away and more."

"And that's no time at all for all the things a lady has to do to complete the arrangements," Deborah replied. "Now straighten yourself up and see if that one area that's too straight can be controlled before it causes embarrassment."

Without realizing it, Anthony had become aroused with his head lying on Deborah's breast. "See what you do to me?" Anthony exclaimed. "You prime my cannon then secure quarters without even allowing a ranging shot."

Deborah giggled as he set to gather himself together to meet his family.

Chapter Twenty-Three

TIME HAD FLOWN BY since *Drakkar* had defeated *Reaper*. Reports had been sent to the Admiralty with several recommendations. Commodore Gardner had favorably endorsed each. It was time Buck and Pope were made captain. Both had held commands and were more than capable to command a frigate. Earl deserved a small command. Maybe he could be made first lieutenant if ever Buck or Pope were promoted.

And Gabe! It had been Gabe in the *Shark* that initiated the assault on the brig that was attacking *Scythe's* stern. He had evaluated the situation, sensed the opportunity, and seized it. Otherwise, had the brig been left unopposed, *Scythe* would have been destroyed or at least overwhelmed right from the start. Gabe's actions not only ensured the outcome of the battle but probably saved a lot of blood. English blood. What would be best for Gabe and Dagan? This was a question Anthony still pondered.

After returning to English Harbour, Anthony had summoned Dagan. In the privacy of his cabin to prevent embarrassment to Dagan, Anthony had thanked him for saving his life. He wanted

Dagan to be assured of his status in the Anthony family. In a quiet moment the two men grasped each other's hand. A knowing and an understanding look passed between the two, and then it was over. The incident had not and would not be mentioned again.

Two new lieutenants had arrived after *Drakkar* had sailed away toward her rendezvous with the *Reaper*. They would have been useful had they arrived earlier but at least they could be of help with so many wounded and killed.

Lieutenant Markham had been placed in command of *LeCroix* after Lieutenant Mainard's death.

Anthony's family had also arrived while *Drakkar* had been sailing toward her rendezvous with the *Reaper*. His sister Becky, her husband Hugh, and little Gretchen (who had grown but was still a spoiled little brat) had all made the trip. Anthony's mother had been too ill to travel, but Gabe's mother, Maria, had made the voyage with Becky and her family. Maria seemed to fit in well enough, and the three women kept the men busy as the wedding day drew near. During one of the few private moments Deborah was able to share with Anthony, she commented, "It's no wonder your father was infatuated with Maria. She's beautiful, sincere, and can be very humorous. At times I'm absolutely jealous."

Gabe spent as much time with his mother as duty allowed, and Anthony was suddenly very glad she came, partly because of Gabe, but also because of Dagan. Dagan had been very subdued ever since the incident with the pirate. Anthony had become worried. However, since Maria had arrived, she and Dagan had spent numerous hours together and he appeared rejuvenated.

Only young Lieutenant Graf, one of the new officers, had been stupid enough to question Dagan's departure from the ship. As Dagan was climbing down to a jolly boat, Graf called to him. "I say Dagan, where are you about?" Dagan's stoic reply was "Ashore." Graf should have dropped it then but didn't. Instead, he said, "I don't recall anyone giving you leave to depart the ship." Anthony had been in conversation with Mr. Stokes, the carpenter, and overheard Graf's remarks. So had Buck.

Not wanting Anthony to be involved, Buck called to Graf. "Excuse me sir, but do you have the watch?"

"Aye, sir," Graf replied to the first lieutenant.

"Well, I wish you'd tend to your duties and leave Dagan to attend his. I declare sir, this watch is as loose as a whore's drawers. I'm not sure you're fit to stand watch over a bumboat."

Stokes grinned at Anthony. "I think Mr. Buck's got the boy's attention, sir. They get to feeling important at that stage and 'as to be taken down a peg or two from time to time."

***

WHEN ANTHONY GOT THE chance to talk private-ly with his sister he asked about their mother. He had the feeling Becky had been hiding something, evading any conversation about their mother. "What is wrong?" he finally demanded.

Becky sighed and said, "Mother's going mad. She goes into fits of delirium. She curses and imagines all sorts of creatures are after her, especially snakes. The doctors give her opium when she's at her worst. Her skin has turned yellow. Jaundiced, the doctors call it. They've bled her, but nothing seems to help, except brandy and the opium."

"It may be the brandy that's caused it," Anthony replied. "I've seen it in a few ship's surgeons."

"Whatever it is," Becky responded, "she can no longer be left alone." Seeing the concern on her brother's face, Becky added, "We're doing all that can be done, Gil. The doctor says it's just a matter of time."

Chapter Twenty-Four

T HE SMALL CHURCH WAS packed. People were even gathered outside around open windows and the back door. The sun was dipping over the horizon, but still the inside of the church was sweltering hot. A heavy haze hung over the anchorage. *So much for a quaint little wedding*, Anthony thought. He was standing at the altar with Gabe as best man beside him. Greta stood opposite to Anthony, as she was Deborah's maid of honor. Watching Deborah walk slowly down the aisle with her escort, Commodore Gardner, made Anthony realize how much he loved this woman. He also realized how lonely his life had been. He'd never be able to put to sea again without regret and concern. He now understood why the Admiralty frowned on young officers getting married.

"Do you, Commodore Lord Gilbert Anthony, Earl of Deerfield, take Lady Deborah McKean?"

"I do."

"Do you, Lady Deborah McKean, take Lord Gilbert Anthony?"

"I do."

"By the powers vested in me by our Holy Father and the Church of England I do hereby pronounce thee man and wife. You may kiss your bride, sir."

When the kiss was complete, the reverend addressed the guests. "I present to you his Lordship and Lady Anthony."

Lieutenant Dunn's marines had turned out as honor guards. Their immaculate dress did much to impress Lady Deborah.

"They're good fighters too," Anthony whispered to his new wife.

The reception at Commodore Gardner's residence seemed to drag on forever. The newlyweds were worn out by the time they'd drunk the evening's last toast.

Deborah was giddy as the carriage took them back to the little cottage where they'd first made love. "Well, you've ruined the gossip for the time being, my husband."

"How so?"

"By making an honest woman of me," she giggled. A certain look came into Deborah's eyes as she nudged still closer to Anthony. "But I'm still as wanton as a tavern wench where you're concerned, sir." Reaching down and grabbing Anthony to add effect, she asked in a coarse whisper, "Are you ready to bed me, sir?" As he became aroused Deborah commented before Anthony could reply. "Oh, me thinks so," she said, trying to mimic Bart.

"Aye, me thinks so indeed," Anthony replied. He was more than ready. They had not made love since his return from the battle with *Reaper*. However, their first night as man and wife made up for the time they'd been apart. Before sleep took Anthony, he whispered to his wife, "A night to remember!"

***

AS BART AND SILAS made their way back to *Drakkar* after the wedding reception was over, they could see the *Royal Chatham* had activity aboard. "They's getting ready to take the newlyweds on their honeymoon I'm bettin'," Bart commented.

"Aye, it appears so," Silas answered. "But what do ye think of 'is Lordship taken us along. They got servants a plenty and a full crew for the *Royal Chatham*."

"What difference do it make why we's going?" Bart answered. "Didn't ye see Lady Deborah's servant girls? They's a pair of lookers, they be. This trip could be like a honeymoon for us if we's able to get them servant girls in a cooperative like mood. What ye think Silas?"

"We'll see mate, we'll see!"

Epilogue

JULY 1775. AS HOT a July as could be remembered on the island of Antigua. Not a person moved during the heat of the day unless it was absolutely necessary. The road from St. Johns all the way to English Harbour was completely empty. Commodores Gardner and Anthony sat in white wicker-backed chairs trying to stay cool as they each drank a glass of chilled lime juice.

The two senior officers listened attentively to the lieutenant before them as he relayed the disturbing news from the colonies. The lieutenant was the commander of the mail packet, *Gull*.

"So it's war," Gardner asked.

"Yes, sir. It appears the talks have failed and we're at war with our own colonies. General Gage, who is the governor of Massachusetts, sent troops to seize weapons that had been cached by the colonials. He was met by a rag tag force. But instead of an open engagement, which General Gage's forces could have easily won, there was a running battle from Lexington to Concord. The colonials carried out one ambush after another. The general's troops finally destroyed the weapons, but reports have it that casualties were very high. Then in June, there was another battle at a place called Bunker Hill. I'm told over fifteen hundred fell that day."

"Damme," snorted Gardner as he got to his feet. "That's a hellish high number. We've not even got started well yet. I told you it'd be a different type of war, did I not sir?"

Gardner directed his comments to Anthony who thus far had listened quietly-but felt disturbed nonetheless.

Gardner invited *Gull's* captain to dine that evening, then had him ushered out. He then turned his attention back to Anthony. "Have you gone through the Admiralty dispatches?"

"Yes," Anthony replied. "I'm to turn *Drakkar* over to Pope. He's been made captain."

"That's a lot of ship for his first command as a captain," Gardner said. "Mine was an old sixth rate twenty-eight gun frigate, and I felt lucky to get her."

"Aye. I remember my first. But Pope has commanded a cutter and a brig. He was first lieutenant on a first rate, and he's shown good judgment since he's been with me. I think he'll do fine. He can keep Steven Earl as his first lieutenant, if he desires. Earl has just about grown up on *Drakkar*, and he's been taught well by Lieutenant Buck and old Peckham."

"Speaking of Buck, why did they not make him captain and give him *Drakkar*?" Gardner quizzed. "He surely deserves it, and he certainly knows the ship."

"That puzzles me as well," Anthony admitted. "My reports strongly recommended Buck for captain and a command. Pope is senior, but Buck should have been made captain long ago. He probably would have, had he not been so loyal to me. This was our second commission together with him as my first lieutenant. At any rate, he's to return to England and report to the Admiralty. I hope they have a ship for him."

"What about you?" Gardner asked.

"I'm to return to England as well, where I'm to report to Lord Sandwich at my earliest convenience."

"You're taking Lady Deborah I'm sure," Gardner commented. "And if she takes a couple of maids, your party will be too big for the packet."

"Yes, I know," Anthony said. "I was thinking of having Gabe take us in the ketch *Shark*. It'll be cramped and rough, but we'll be a private ship." Anthony then looked at his friend and knew he'd miss him. "What have you decided?" Anthony asked.

"I haven't yet," Gardner replied. "There's sure to be another admiral take command of the station, and I doubt he'll be as genteel as Sir Lawrence was."

"You may be placed in command of a squadron, or maybe even given your flag," Anthony said, trying to be optimistic for his friend.

"No, I'm to long behind a desk to be given a

squadron. I've been in the Indies too long to have enough influence to even be considered for anything important. No, I'll stay as dockyard commissioner as long as they'll let me. The truth is that before the hostilities erupted I was going to retire from government service, move to Virginia in the colonies, and go into shipping with a friend. But now who knows?"

***

LONDON WAS BUSTLING, AND Lady Deborah was astonished at the pace of things. The voyage back to England had been very pleasant and uneventful. When Anthony and Gabe returned to the Admiralty for their appointment there was a definite change. The lazy ho-hum attitude had been replaced with a sense of urgency. Gabe didn't seem as overwhelmed as he did that first trip. He was older now-a lieutenant and a mature, seasoned officer. A veteran of several ship-to-ship actions, and he carried the scars to prove it. There were admirals here in Whitehall who hadn't seen the action that Gabe had. Anthony had noticed some of the looks they'd received upon entering the Admiralty. Gabe's black hair now had a long narrow strip of gray where a bullet had grazed his scalp. Anthony knew Gabe was sensitive about "his streak." Deborah had told him it made him look not only handsome, but also mysterious and romantic.

Overhearing the comment, Caleb had let out a groan and stated, "God woman, don't give him anymore reason to lord his prowess over us mortals."

One of the clerks greeted Anthony and Gabe, and assured them the first lord would be with them directly. As soon as the clerk was out of earshot, Gabe whispered to Anthony, "'Cept for the glasses, don't he favor Caleb's ape?"

Anthony's burst of laughter caused stares from other officers. But damme if Gabe wasn't right. The resemblance was there. The clerk returned quickly, somewhat disturbed by Anthony's chuckling. The clerk was used to a more somber attitude from those officers who entered this hallowed place.

"The First Lord will see you now," the clerk said as he directed Anthony and Gabe to Lord Sandwich's office.

"Gil! How nice to see you again. And you as well Gabe. Well Gil, you've done your duty as I knew you would. In this time of gloom you've been my ray of sunshine. I knew you were the man to handle those pirates. Your deeds have not gone unnoticed. That, I promise you. Nor have yours, Gabe," the First Lord added.

Turning, Lord Sandwich bid a clerk to come forward. "This gentlemen is Evan Nepean. He is my head clerk. I don't know what I'd do without him. He has orders for both of you that you can sign for before you leave. But first I want to chat a while and fill you in on what's awaiting you. I've already told you I'm proud of both of you. My political light doesn't shine as it once did. But I want you both to know if I can ever be of service to either of you, all you have to do is call upon me. The papers have been full of stories of your engagements and triumphs. The papers call you the 'Fighting Anthonys.' I can't count the times you've made *The Gazette*. There's even wagering at the club as to how fat your purses have grown."

Sensing Anthony's need to say something modest, the First Lord waved his hand. "Nay, Nay. Don't be concerned."

"It's good. A man should be rewarded for his pains. And by the bye, I almost forgot, not only did you capture a bunch of damn pirates but also I hear you've succeeded in capturing a lovely lady's heart. Here's my hand in congratulations. I look forward to meeting her."

"Thank you, My Lord," Anthony replied, sensing the formalities were over and it was now time for business.

"I know you both are aware that we are now at war with the Colonies. Several senior officers have chosen not to fight their American cousins. Lord Keppel is among them. Truth be known, I'm not sure I blame them, the way Lord North is running things. However, so many senior officers retiring rather than fighting has in some ways been a blessing. We are now able to promote several deserving officers into commands that otherwise would have been difficult." Having said this, Lord Sandwich walked over to Anthony and said,

"Let me be the first to congratulate you on your promotion to Rear Admiral. I know your father would have been as proud as I am. On your recommendation, we've promoted Buck to captain and he's been given command of *Merlin*, a thirty-two gun frigate. *Merlin* will be under your flag. Her previous captain is one of those that decided he'd pursue parliament rather than fight the colonials. In regards to Buck, I know you would have liked to have him as your flag captain, but he was too junior to command a ship of the line. Your flagship will be the *Warrior*. She's a seventy-four that was launched in 1770 at Chatham. She has just undergone complete overhaul and refitting. She's awaiting you at Portsmouth. Her captain is an old friend of yours, Dutch Moffitt. A hellish fine officer who will hoist his own flag someday."

"Now for you, my young firebrand," Lord Sandwich said directing his attention to Gabe. "We have, in fact, captured a privateer, the *Sea Wolf*. The Americans originally planned her as a slaver, but before she was completed she was converted to a privateer. She was to be a predator as her name invokes. She is a sleek ship I'm told, and mounts sixteen guns. Normally, such a vessel would go to one more senior. However, few lieutenants have seen the action you have, and at this point in time England needs experienced officers to make up for inept politicians. Admiral, Lieutenant, I shan't detain you any longer. You have my faith and trust. You'll do your duty as you always have. I know I can count on you. Pick up your orders from Evan on your way out. Now be off with you. Go celebrate with your wife and families, and then report to your commands as directed by your orders."

"WE HAVE A WAR TO FIGHT!"